PEREGRINATION

THE JOURNEY TO WELLNESS

SONNY WEATHERSBY

PEREGRINATION

THE JOURNEY TO WELLNESS

SONNY WEATHERSBY

Peregrination: The Journey to Wellness

Published in 2018 by Big League Publishing

Library of Congress-in-Publications-Data

Printed in the United States of America

10 9 8 7 6 5 4 3 2 1

ISBN: 978-1-7335617-0-9

Table of Contents

Prologue 7

Chapter 1: Humble Beginnings................................. 11

Chapter 2: Putting on a Performance....................... 19

Chapter 3: On the Run 27

Chapter 4: What's Your Name, Kid?........................ 41

Chapter 5: Growing Pains.. 49

Chapter 6: A Family in Prayer................................. 59

Chapter 7: Keeping My Promise.............................. 63

Chapter 8: Baseball Years.. 81

Chapter 9: Prime Time... 97

Chapter 10: The Stage.. 115

Chapter 11: 9/11 129

Chapter 12: Salute.. 139

Chapter 13: The Mark of a Soldier 149

Epilogue 153

With definiteness of purpose, goals, and a plan of action, anything can be achieved.

Prologue

I began running every morning trying to ease the pain and frustration. My life was in complete chaos, and I was in need of an answer from God. I was searching for peace.

This particular morning was the beginning of that answer - it was my awakening.

It was 6:30A.M. on a Tuesday, and I was dressed in my typical running attire - sweats, basketball shorts, a white t-shirt under my hoodie, and a gray beanie that read BOXING in the front. There was no doubt that I had the ferocity of a fighter in my eyes. But, I had yet to make my transition into the ring.

Twenty minutes had passed and while jogging with my headphones on, a lady ran up to me frantically and said, "Young man, young man, did you just hear the news? The Afghani's bombed the World Trade Center!" It hadn't dawned on me what she said. I continued jogging, but in retrospect, I was a dead man running. I was too entrenched in my own self-pity and disillusionment to take it all in.

When I finally made it home, my grandmother and all her employees were sitting in front of the TV looking at news repeats of the airplanes flying into the WTC.

"Sonny, you hear the news?" my Grandma CJ asked. "Baby, it's the end of the world, just what they been talking about in the book of Revelation. We needs to repent! Gawd is coming back!"

I stood in silence as I watched buildings collapse, hundreds of bodies carried out by firefighters, skies filled with gray, and tears shedding by the pound. At this moment, I just needed a cool shower to reflect on all that was going on. It was difficult to grasp that something of this magnitude actually happened. After taking it all in, all I could think about were the families and friends of the loved ones left behind to grieve. This was something I knew far too well.

I took this global attack very personally. This was not about being rich or poor, a failure or success, neither black nor white—it was about being an American. There was no way you could have lived in this country and not felt the pain and agony of these terroristic events. For the first time in my life, I identified with something greater than my own plight.

As a kid, we all have dreams and aspirations to become something great in life – an entertainer, a doctor, a lawyer, or maybe an athlete, just to name a few. Many of us reach our dreams, and many of us don't. But, like all dreams, they too must come to an end. At the end of the day, we all have to be prepared for what's next. Where do we go from here? Do we sit and blame our situations on our circumstances? Or, do we aspire for change? Change alone takes tremendous faith and courage, and without the support from loved ones and peers, it's almost impossible to do so. Inevitably, maturation is a constant journey…peregrination.

In 1980, 40% of African-American families were led by single parents.

Chapter 1

Humble Beginnings

It was early Monday morning, late August 1980, my twin sister, Linda, my big brother, Bo, and I sat at the breakfast table. We were waiting on LaVassa, my eldest sister, to prepare our breakfast cereal. My mom was pregnant with my baby sister, Cupcake, at the time. Today was extra special because it was Linda's and my first day of kindergarten and because Bo let me open the box of cereal and have the toy inside.

"You're officially a big boy today," said Bo. "You scared?" "No, I'm ready," I said.

Looking across at my twin, I had noticed she was quiet the entire morning. I knew she was nervous.

"Linda's scared," said LaVassa, as she poured the milk into my bowl.

"You'll be alright, sis," said Bo.

Linda barely uttered a word at the table.

Bo whispered, "Remember what I told you, bro? If anyone touches you or Linda, you make sure you punch them square in the nose."

"Yep, I remember. I ain't scared. I just can't wait to see the girls!"

"You too little to be worrying about girls, boy," said my mom walking into the kitchen. "Hurry up, we gottta get ready to leave," she asserted.

I rushed and finished my cereal first. I knew there was a whole world waiting for me, and I was ready to conquer it.

That morning, Bo went over everything he taught me so I could be prepared for kindergarten. He taught me the Pledge of Allegiance, the alphabet, and how to count. Surprisingly, the alphabet and counting was tough, but the Pledge of Allegiance I knew well and couldn't wait to say it in class.

Bo was my mom's younger sister's son, who had him when she was fourteen years old. She thought it'd be best for my mom to raise him since he was only a year younger than LaVassa. This also would give her time to mature and get on her feet. Bo was technically my mom and dad's first son, my brother.

My mom dropped LaVassa and Bo off first. He was starting 2nd grade and LaVassa was beginning 3rd grade. Looking back now, they both seemed so much older and mature. I guess when you're five years old everything seems so much bigger.

My mom walked Linda and me to class that morning. "You make sure you look after your twin sister," she said.

"I will mom," I said.

* * *

Five minutes after entering class, the bell rang. The teacher introduced herself and said, "The very first thing we do before class starts is recite the Pledge of Allegiance. Does anyone know the Pledge of Allegiance?"

A few other students raised their hand, but I attracted the most attention erratically leaping from my chair. "Me, me, me!"

The teacher called on me, "And who might you be young man?"

"My name is Sonny Howard Weathers III."

"Wow! What a dignified name you have." I smiled.

"Now class, Mr. Weathers is going to be leading us in the Pledge of Allegiance. Ready? Begin."

"I pledge allegiance to the flag of the United States of America..." I said it perfectly and couldn't have been prouder.

* * *

Looking back, Bo and LaVassa were like parents to me, but I must admit I am truly my parents' son. I got my outgoing personality from my dad, and without a doubt, I possess my mother's strength. She is the strongest woman I know.

My mom had always been a stickler for education. She believed that education was the key to liberation and economic progress. My mom was raised during The Black

Power Movement and post-Civil Rights Era, when the oppression of blacks was common in society. Her parents lived during segregation and her great grandparents were slaves, so my mom was a very proud woman. Born and raised in Watts, California, she had to be strong to face all the negativity and oppression in her community. She never backed down from a fight, and she took nothing from no one.

Born to Hank and Minnie Pearl Robinson in 1953, my mom was the eldest of 11 children. She never had the chance to experience the fruits of her youth because her mother became ill when she was ten years old. Pain, disappointment and misery struck my mother at an early age. Five years later, when my mom was only fifteen years old, her mother died.

A year prior to that, her father left the home because he could not handle running a business and taking care of his sick wife and eleven kids. My mom never spoke badly about her father. In fact, she said he was a good man and didn't blame him for leaving. She always told us that he did the best he could to give his family a good life.

Before my grandmother's death, she asked my mom to take care of her siblings and to be strong for the family. After she passed, her grandmother took her in and her 10 siblings. By the time my mom was seventeen, her grandmother had remarried, relocated out the state, and decided it was best that the kids be separated and raised by different family members.

My dad, Sonny Weathers Jr., was born in 1953 to Carol and Sonny Weathers Sr. My dad was born in Fresno, California and was the eldest of five brothers and sisters. Word has it that Sonny Sr. was an abusive drunk. His mom wanted a better life for them, so she left him for a local evangelist whom she felt would be a better man to raise her children. They married and relocated to Los Angeles in the 1960's. My dad didn't talk much about his youth except for the fact that he had to work at his family business. He told me he wanted to be an athlete when he was young, but due to his heavy workload, he was unable to participate. My dad grew up in Hancock Park, an upper-class neighborhood in L.A. Most would say he grew up privileged, but what's wealth when you're plagued with being away from your biological father? My mom believed this lead to his early alcohol and drug abuse.

My parents met in church when my dad was sixteen and my mom was fifteen. My mom always tells the story of how my dad told her that she was going to be his wife and the mother of his children when they first met. It would appear that my parents were the perfect match, being that they were both young, good-looking, crazy about each other, and in some ways opposites. My mom was the strength that my father needed in a woman - someone that would listen and understand his heart. A good Christian woman to uphold the morals and values his mom taught him. My dad was my mother's knight and shining armor. He was not the typical man she was used to seeing in her neighborhood. He was awkward, but clean-cut and well-spoken. Nevertheless, their union was meant to be. It was more than just words spoken. Years later, they married and had four children.

More than 150,000 children will likely spend time in a juvenile facility.

Chapter 2

Putting on a Performance

The summer of '83 was one to remember. The house was full of family. Bo stayed the entire time, along with my aunt Boosie and older cousin Holly, who watched over us while my mom worked all day and night. My dad was not around much during this time, but those years were probably the best years in my life. We were like the Little Rascals, always getting into stuff.

It's true when they say kids who grow up with older siblings mature faster. I had learned everything about being a kid from my brother and sister, especially Bo, who I wanted to be just like.

That summer, LaVassa had organized all the kids in the neighborhood to put on the performance *The Dreamgirls,* inspired from the Broadway play. LaVassa got the idea from Holly. She was her protégée. She got all the kids in the neighborhood to participate, and we practiced for weeks. It was an all-girls show, but the boys were responsible for production.

The day of the show, we set the garage up like a stage, with curtains, and we set up chairs for the audience. We had passed out flyers a week before the event, and it seemed like the whole neighborhood showed up, parents as well as kids.

The show started at 6:00P.M., right around the same time my mom came home. She had no idea what we had done because we wanted to surprise her. We wanted to show her how innovative we were.

As my mom pulled up from work, we had Bo meet her at her car and walk her to the backyard, which was already full of people. My mom's initial response was, "What are all these people doing in my yard?" But Bo was the perfect person to get her to calm down. My mom could never be mad at Bo.

Bo walked her to the front row where we prepared her a seat and the show started. During the intermission, we served food and drinks, and every member of our family performed. Bo was the DJ rocking to the tunes of the Jackson 5 and Michael Jackson, who was hot that year. Linda sang a song, with LaVassa playing the keyboards. Bo also played the guitar, and I was on the drums that I made from cardboard boxes and trashcans. We were actually pretty good. The entire show was a success. We received a standing ovation from our neighbors, and my mom smiled so big that day because of our performance. My mom never smiled much, so we were all ecstatic just to see her smile.

My mom never asked us where we got the money to pay for the costumes and production. Nor would any of us dare to tell her. LaVassa organized a plan that we dress up in our Boy and Girl Scout outfits, and go door to door to raise the money. I know now that it was not the "right" thing to do, but as kids, no one questioned it. Bo and I, and our buddy, Dwayne, from next door who stuttered when he spoke, went door to door with a pitch that Bo created.

"Excuse me sir or ma'am, we're from the Boy Scouts of America, and we are seeking money for our charity to help underprivileged boys and girls in our community."

It was Bo's idea to let Dwayne speak. He figured it would be perfect because the people would feel sorry for him because of his speech impediment. Dwayne could never remember his lines, and he stuttered so bad that people would just go to their wallets and put money in the bucket, without him even finishing what he was trying to say. In a week, we raised over $200. The next day, we threw an ice-cream party for all the kids who participated in the show with the leftover money we raised.

* * *

That summer I finally learned how to swim, I got my first kiss, and I mastered the art of hustling by going door to door whenever I needed extra cash in my Boy Scouts uniform. If the boys weren't up to that, we would walk down to the local grocery store and make a little change helping people with their groceries and returning the carts early in the morning. Bo always made sure we made $5 each so we had enough money to go to the local swimming pool and have lunch afterwards.

My brother Bo was only 10 at the time, but he was tall for his age and usually dated girls that were older than he was. Bo hooked me up with his girlfriend Carla's little sister, Marlene. Carla was twelve, and Marlene was ten. Marlene was young but experienced; she had already gone to third base with a guy. I was very shy and Marlene was more experienced than I was. She was the one to make the first move—she taught me how to kiss. I did not let her know that she was the first person I kissed, so I just went along with it. She grabbed me close and put my hand on her butt, and said with a Spanish accent, "This is the way guys do it." Though she was only ten, she seemed voluptuous. She already had breasts. She let me rub her breasts, and when I made a move to touch her in other places, like Bo had told me to do, she stopped me and said, "I can't because I'm on my period." I had no idea what that even meant, so we continued kissing and grinding until it was time to go.

I had later asked Bo what it means when a girl says she is on her period. He told me, "It's when a girl bleeds from her private." Just the thought made me sick. I promised myself I was going to wait until I was married to have sex.

Towards the end of the summer, Bo's mom was starting to get on her feet, and she wanted him to move back in with her before school started. She had even started the process of having him transferred to a school in Carson. I knew life was going to be different for me from that point on.

His last day home with us, we both cried; as a matter a fact, we all did, including my mom. He wiped my eyes and said, "Don't trip. I'm gonna run away and come back." For some reason, I felt like him moving out of our house was the last time I would see him, but Bo kept his word. By the time school started in the fall, he had run away from his mom in

Carson a few times to come back to our house. He caught the bus on his own, but my mom always took him back even though he begged her to stay.

By September, Bo had to go to juvenile hall (juvie) for stealing and skipping school. Since that was his first offense, he was going to get out in time for Christmas.

* * *

My dad, who had been out running the streets, came back to live with us around Christmas time as well, and I was so happy. I was happy to have my dad around because I wanted to get to know him, and I didn't have to be the only guy in the house. My dad was absent from our home for periods of time because he and my mom used to fight about the lifestyle he was living, but I still looked up to him. He was a big and strong man that I still desired to be like in some ways. I was too young to understand that my dad was simply a functioning alcoholic and drug user at that point.

That Christmas was most memorable because our entire family was together, and everyone was happy. My mom cooked everything imaginable, and my dad really came through big with the presents. My dad had gotten me everything I wanted. Most importantly was two pairs of boxing gloves, a pair for me and a pair for Bo. Whatever my dad got me, he bought Bo. Bo and I took pictures in front of the Christmas tree with our gloves. We spent the entire Christmas day boxing.

Though my brother never spoke about his time in juvie to me, I was just happy to have my brother and my dad back in my life. I never wanted them to leave me again, and for a little while, I was still able to see them often enough to keep my hopes of us all living together again.

Over 20 million Americans over the age of 12 have a drug/alcohol addiction.

Chapter 3

On the Run

That great feeling I had during Christmas quickly faded by the following year. I thought that my boxing gloves were an indication that my dad would start taking me to the boxing gym soon since he was the first person to introduce me to boxing.

He would pick me up and take me to his buddy's house to watch the major fights. The most memorable were the "Sugar Ray" Leonard vs. Duran "No Mas" fight and the "Sugar Ray" vs. Hurnes fight in '81. It was my dad's dream that I became a boxer, and he promised me that he would start my lessons at the local gym. I was just happy about the idea of my father and me sharing something together. However, my boxing gloves became dust collectors, hanging on the edge of my bed as my dad just continued to be in and out of our house.

Bo started to come around less and less and began embracing the street life in Carson. I started to get into trouble in school for fighting. I guess my anger ignited when Bo went back to juvenile hall, along with the fights between my parents - stemming from my dad's drug and alcohol binges. Times were getting rough, and the tension and arguing between my parents escalated to an all-time high. I began to regret my dad being around. He was not working, and his new addiction forced him to start pawning and selling everything from the house and stealing money from my mom constantly. My mom was the only one who worked and was trying to pay the mortgage alone, and it was tough. Many times, my mom barely had money for food. If it were not for the lunch ticket program at school, we would have gone many days without eating at all. Every time my dad would come home, he was either drunk or high. It was so bad my siblings and I used to wish he would just not come home at all.

My dad's only concern at this point was getting money to keep getting high. We were all so terrified of our dad that my sisters and I would hide in the room together with the door locked. My youngest sister, Cupcake, was too young to understand what was going on half the time, and when the fighting took place, she would just cry. LaVassa would do her best to try to console her. Most of the time, Linda would hide in the closet, and LaVassa and I would be too scared to do or say anything. We would just hear the loud bangs and screams from our room.

One night my mom decided to lock my dad out of the house. I guess she was sick and tired of the fighting.

"LaVassa, if your dad comes back tonight, don't let him in. If he acts crazy, call the cops."

We knew that night would not end well when we heard him yelling and kicking the door from outside our window. He cussed and called my mom every name in the book, and we just prayed that he would not get through the door...he did. We heard a loud BOOM! It was the sound of the back door that lead to her room being kicked in. He had locked us out of her bedroom. The screaming and yelling immediately followed. My father was hysterical. He was throwing everything around as he yelled at my mom to give him some damn money.

She screamed back, "I don't have any money. Why don't you just leave, Howard?" They tussled and were fighting over my mom's purse. "Give me my purse." We listened and could feel and hear every blow to our mother's face and body. We just cried and tried not to make any noise.

My older sister LaVassa ran and dialed 911, but hung up without saying anything. The cops came ten minutes later, but my mom lied and told them everything was OK. We were hurt and confused why our mom never made the police take him away when she had the chance. We would just cry to ourselves because it never failed. We'd have to listen to them fighting and her crying, then we would hear them in bed hours after their fights. To add insult to injury, my mom would prepare food for my dad afterwards. I mean we barely had enough food in the house for us. I began to hate being home, as this routine became the norm in my house.

The morning after these episodes, I would often watch my mom attempt to cover up the truth about what was going on in her house. When she applied her makeup, it was as if she was trying to erase the pain and bruises. But, it was simply her way of covering up the embarrassment that came from her being an abused woman. I knew she was embarrassed to go to work and church with her scars and

29

bruises. In the professional and church world, my mom was perceived as a strong and intelligent woman, so of course no one could understand why she chose to stay around the chaos and ignorance that came from my dad. It simply did not make sense why she continued to put up with him.

The fighting and chaos would keep us up in the wee hours of the night, so we were often sleepy on school mornings. One could only imagine how our home life started to affect our schoolwork. This life began to change my mom as a person and as a mother. My mother was not very affectionate to begin with, so the few smiles or hugs that we would get on occasion became obsolete by the time the abuse picked up. Instead of showing us more love, giving more kisses, and trying to be the emotional escape we needed as children, my mother became the complete opposite.

Her voice grew cold and stern, and she became more physical with us. She had no patience and tolerance for what she considered 'childish.' It felt like she began taking out her frustrations of being poor and abused on us. Her actions were that black and white. She began communicating with us the way our father communicated with her. She began using angry and hurtful words to express herself. I started to despise her telling me, "You're just like your dad, you little punk." And, if I did not behave 'manly' enough in her eyes, she did not refrain from calling me "punk." I was heartbroken by my mother, really did my best to please her and did not understand why she took her anger out on me.

My sisters experienced their fair share of this abuse as well. The more hurtful things she said and did to me, the more it made me hate my father. At the end of the day, I blamed him for the way my mother treated my sisters and me.

* * *

For a long period in my life, I was three different people. I was a frightened kid in the home, a good boy in church, and a nemesis on the schoolyard. I was prone to wetting the bed every now and again, but when the abuse was its highest in our home, I started wetting the bed on a regular basis. To solve this problem, one time my mom made me wear a diaper to school. I was convinced that my mother wanted me to feel the shame and embarrassment she felt from my father, and she was on a mission to make me suffer - and no one could tell me different.

"Why did you hit that kid, Sonny? You know your mom is going to have a meeting with the principal," explained my elementary teacher as she escorted me down the hall. As I walked down the hall, the tears rolled down my cheeks, not because I was scared of being suspended, but because my mom had put the fear of God in me and had warned me that if I were to get in trouble again, I would get the whooping of my life. When I got to the principal's office I was somewhat relieved I got there before my mom. I was hoping I would be able to convince them it wasn't my fault this time.

"He called me pissy boy and was talking about the holes in my shoes," I told the principal and counselor.

Then the counselor asked, "Why did he call you that name?"

"My mom made me wear a diaper to school to teach me not to pee in the bed," I replied.

"She made you wear a diaper?" she asked.

"Yes," I responded. She proceeded to take notes.

She then said, "Some teachers have told me that you're falling asleep in class and that you have come to class with marks on your body. Is there something going on at home that you want to tell us about?"

I lied, "No, there isn't anything going on at home. I just had to wear a diaper because I pee in the bed." Moments later, my mom walked in, and the counselor and principal asked her the same questions.

She told them, "I am doing the best I can to provide and make sure my kids get a good education. I don't condone bad behavior. I do not want my kids to end up arrested or in no juvenile system. I am doing my best to raise four kids on my own. I am not asking for any sympathy. I just want you to understand I don't tolerate any kind of misbehavior from my children."

The counselor told my mom, "He was more than likely acting out in school because something was going on in the house. We are not sure what, Mrs. Weathers, but it needs to be taken seriously."

"I do take it seriously," my mother said defensively. "And my kids are getting the best from me."

"Well, Mrs. Weathers, we are not going to suspend Sonny this time, but he cannot continue to fight in school," said the principal.

"Ma'am, I will do my best to make sure it doesn't happen again."

Boy did I just dodge a bullet. I was so elated I almost had an out of body experience when the principal uttered those words. I knew I had avoided the worst whooping in my life. By the end of the meeting and to my surprise, my mother was not very angry with me. She whispered sternly, "Go to class, and don't let me have to come back up here."

My mother was also very keen on sharing her wisdom. She wanted us to understand the harsh realities of the world and our life around us, even though we were too young to understand. She instilled us with the 'truths' about the world. She explained that black people came from nothing, so we would have to strive to be great in life if we wanted to amount to anything. She would keep us up many nights talking about her life and her views about what we needed to do in this life to make it out of the rut we were born into.

"My great grandparents were slaves, and *they* had it hard. My great grandfather was beaten while he watched his wife being raped. They had to live through slavery, and I had to live through periods of discrimination. Y'all kids don't know how good y'all got it. I'll be darned if y'all go to school and mess your lives up. I work too hard every day to keep this family together."

She gave this lecture so much my sister and I would mock her jokingly when she took her eyes off us. We did whatever we could to make light of the situation. If we dared to fall asleep during one of her lectures, she would wake us up with a slap across the face. "Wake up, boy. Falling asleep? That's what's wrong with black people today. They sleep on the realities of life. Black people need to wake up."

I guess she wanted us to rationalize why we had to go through what we were going through and that life was hard. But, we were kids. We were young, and we just wanted to be kids.

* * *

By the time I was 11, things had gotten out of hand. Our family and church knew about the abuse in our home. My mom decided she had enough because she was losing us. We moved to Watts, CA with my mom's church friend, Gina. The Sunday prior to us moving, she went to church wearing shades, and that was the talk of the church. All the women in the church gathered around my mom and prayed for her. She was a young 33-year-old woman and did not deserve what she was going through.

Gina was gracious enough to let my mom and us in her home. We left everything behind, with the exception of a few outfits. My mom promised us that she would get it together, and we wouldn't have to go through that abuse again. We were all happy to get away from our dad and begin a new life.

One time I was listening in on Gina telling my mom, "You don't need to be exposing your kids to that kind of abuse, and you can stay here as long as you need." My mom did not respond, but I was just happy someone was telling my mom to stay away from my dad.

My mom's friend had a son, Jimmy. He was around my age, so I was looking forward to having another boy around. We moved into her apartment around the summertime, and it was very crammed. There were about ten people living in the 2-bedroom apartment, so privacy was just nonexistent. On top of that, the rats and roaches had made a comfortable place for themselves in the apartment too. We made the best of it, and honestly, we were rarely there. On one hand, I was grateful that my mom's friend let us live with her; but on the other hand, I hated living in that apartment.

Jimmy introduced me to all the kids in the neighborhood, which made my transformation to Watts life a little easier. The kids in the neighborhood thought that I talked "white" and was soft, but after a few street fights with the neighborhood kids, I proved that I was no punk. My Boy Scout skills started to come in handy, and I was now one of the cool kids.

Our mom kept us enrolled in school on the Westside of L.A. We had to catch the bus on our own every morning by 6:00A.M. from Watts to the Westside to be on time for school. I now had roaches coming out of my bags in class, so that just gave the kids in school something else to tease me about.

I didn't pay too much attention to them teasing me because my life in Watts was not filled with all the drama we'd grown used to. Even though our commute to school was tough and our mom still did not have much, I still managed to pull my grades out the gutter. I was in the top of my 6th grade class that fall semester.

* * *

During the week, we would go to our grandmother's house after school and wait for my mom to pick us after work to go back to Watts. Often times, when my mom picked us up from my grandmother's house, we were headed to church. We were going to Bible Study, choir rehearsal (I was the church drummer), and revival. My sister and I really enjoyed it too because we could meet up with all our cousins on my mom's side, family, and friends.

Being at church, I really looked forward to spending time with my older cousin Michael, whom Bo and I called Big Mike. He was around the same age as Bo and whenever Bo was around, you could guarantee to find the three of us together. As the youngest, I had to prove I was tough enough to hang, so Big Mike and Bo would always challenge me to

36

fight the other boys in church. Big Mike was the pastor's son, but when we were together, he would let loose. Having both of my big bros around made me feel invincible, and I would have fought anyone to keep it that way. I did not see Big Mike much outside of church because he didn't live in L.A., so I cherished the time we did have in church, especially when Bo wasn't around.

By this time, our church choir was becoming popular around the city. My sisters sang in the choir, and I was starting to get paid to play the drums. The church had even bought me a new drum set, so I wanted very much to be there as often as I could. Going to church and playing the drums were the best ways for me to clear my mind.

* * *

My dad didn't know where we were staying, but he knew he could always find us at church. One day he secretly followed us from church to Gina's house. A few minutes after we all got in the apartment, we heard a knock at the door. It was him.

Gina yelled, "She doesn't want you here, Howard."

My dad yelled back, "Well, I just want to talk to my wife!"

My mom rushed to the door and walked outside to talk to my dad, and when she came back inside, we knew he had sucked her back into his game. She happily told us, "Well, he found us a 2-bedroom apartment in our old neighborhood!"

Though I wasn't thrilled to move back to the possibility of all the drama, I was happy to get away from the rats and roaches.

More than 380 gang-related killings took place in Los Angeles County in 1987.

Chapter 4

What's Your Name, Kid?

Early in 1987, we moved to our new apartment in Mid-City Los Angeles. It was an upgrade from Watts, but far less than what we were used to growing up in our old home. Mid-City was the borderline of where wealth and poverty met.

It wasn't too long before my dad was back to his old tricks - drinking, doing drugs, chasing women, and being absent from my life. He even missed my elementary school graduation, which highlighted me graduating with honors and giving a speech, "If You Believe, Success Will Come." With all the moving and all the chaos that was going on, I was somehow able to stay focused.

Now that I was back on the Westside, I was around my old childhood friends who were now members of the local neighborhood gang. Growing up in L.A., young men are often times associated with the gangs around their neighborhood. It's difficult and almost impossible to grow up in areas and not be associated. You're affiliated either by having friends who are gang members or just by your zip code. To be in a gang meant that not only were you down to protect the integrity of the neighborhood, or hood, but you were all about getting money. That's what I was all about.

Forced to become the man of my house, I had adult responsibilities going into junior high school. I knew from

Bo that hanging out in the streets would only get me locked up, so I decided to hustle whatever I could get my hands on. I used to bring two duffel bags everywhere I went filled with candy, collectible coins, comic books, baseball cards, and my mom's Avon products, which I sold to the teachers at school.

Later that summer I got a job at Audrey's, a local barbershop in my neighborhood. Audrey usually employed the young kids to come to sweep up, dust, windex the mirrors, etc. But I came in there and set up shop. I sold candy and snacks, shined shoes, swept hair, sold my mom's Avon's products, and made store runs for customers. I was able to help my mom with the money I made at Audrey's along with all my other hustles. I saved up enough money to buy my own school clothes that fall. Working at the barbershop, I was around a lot of pimps, players, gangsters and hustlers from our neighborhood.

"What's your name, kid?" asked Chu-Chu, a known hustler and drug dealer.

"They call me Sonny," I said.

"This kid reminds me of me when I was little, huh Audrey?" asked Chu-Chu.

Audrey said, "Not even close, boy!" She told Chu-Chu I was much smarter than he was and that I came to work *every* day. Everyone laughed.

Chu-Chu told me that as a kid, he used to work at Audrey's.

"He going to be a hustler when he grows up," he said emphatically. "I can tell."

"I don't think so!" she replied. "I can see him being a lawyer or something prestigious. He's a smart kid with a good head on his shoulders."

She turned to me and said, "You study hard in school and make something of your life. Ain't nothing wrong with an honest hustle, but the wrong kind of hustling leads to a life of crime."

"Well hustling ain't been bad for me," as Chu-Chu pulled out big wads of money from his socks and pockets. "I only got a 10th grade education, kid, and life's been good." He smiled.

As a 12-year-old, I was impressed. I had never seen anyone with that much money before. I respected Audrey and her words because she only had a high school education herself, and she had run a successful business for years on the Westside of L.A.

I was saddened to hear that Chu-Chu died later that summer. Word was that he was robbed and killed. Looking back, I often wondered why he chose the life he did. He was streetwise, had the gift of gab and was well liked. I'm sure he could have been anything he wanted in life.

* * *

Fall of '87 was the first time my twin and I were separated. Due to her singing endeavors, Linda went to a performing arts school, and I went to John Burroughs Junior High with all my friends. Junior high was a big transition for me socially, but thanks to my fighting reputation, I was able to gain some popularity among the in crowd. I got into a fight my first day of school with an 8th grader who was bullying other 7th graders on the basketball court after class. I was fighting for my respect and for my hood. I whooped him up pretty good. Word spread around campus fast that I wasn't the one to be messed with.

I never strayed too far from my focus and the confidence Audrey had in me. I wanted to be something great, but I wasn't too sure how because I really didn't have confidence in myself academically. However, I still believed that my life was somehow destined for greatness. I was not going to allow myself to fall weak to the minor stresses other kids were dealing with, like being popular and wearing name brand clothes.

I was also beginning to gain an identity as a baseball player in junior high. The summer before 8th grade, I played my first year of little league baseball. I made the All-Star team my first year playing, and this was the beginning of my athletic prowess. I found myself hanging around the nerds, the kids who were baseball fans collecting baseball cards. My love for baseball and the LA Dodgers began to grow as well, and I never missed a game thanks to AM 790. Learning the game was inevitable with Vin Scully on the radio. He became like a surrogate father to me, and his words of wisdom and guidance kept me away from trouble.

That summer of 1988, my Uncle T, my mom's brother, came to live with us. Bo also came around sporadically when he wasn't running the streets. My Uncle T and Bo were the only ones who took me to all of my games because my mom worked two jobs and my dad was not around. While Bo had completely given his life to the streets, I was on my own path to pursuing my dream of becoming a major-league baseball player.

By the end of the summer, Bo was facing some serious time in juvie for a drug possession charge. Around the same time, my Uncle T was headed to prison for violating his parole.

* * *

I still found happiness amidst everything that was going on in my life.

That year the Dodgers won the World Series and thanks to my mom's Avon products and my grades being up, I had gained some favoritism from all the teachers. I was one of the kids selected from my school to go to a Dodger Banquet at the Bonaventure Hotel downtown. This was the highlight of my life. I now knew what I wanted to do with my life, and this experience solidified my desire to be a professional baseball player. I was going to do everything I could to make that happen.

That summer before high school in '89, my mom moved us to West Covina to run away from my dad once again. We moved in with her younger sister in a really nice condo. Bo got out early due to technicalities and good behavior, so he was also living with my auntie at that time. It also helped that my auntie Viola was director of the juvenile hall. LaVassa stayed with my grandmother in L.A. and would come visit on some weekends. So, it was just me, my twin and Cupcake.

Bo and I were back together again. It was like the good old times. We went to the malls to check out the girls, went swimming, played video games, and played baseball the entire summer. He was excited about me getting ready to play in high school. We would talk for hours about what we would do when I made it to the pros. Although Bo was heavy in the gang life, nothing changed between us - around me, he could joke, play, and be that big kid I knew he really was.

"Alright, let's see what you got, kid," he said staring at me at the plate. He stood at a high 6'1", the same size as most big- league pitchers, with a fastball in the high 80s. I waited for him to deliver the next pitch, a fastball.

CRACK...a home run!

"You wearing me out, kid! Man, you ready for high school now!"

Every pitch he threw for a strike, I would CRACK over the fence.

"It ain't like the old days, Bo. I been practicing," I said. "I see!" Bo exclaimed.

"This is where the next pitch is going," as I pointed to the fence.

CRACK...another home run!

"My arm is done, kid! I can't throw anymore." Packing up, as we were ready to go, he said, "I see you're going to do great!"

"Naw, bro. *We're* going to do great! I can't do it without you."

"I'm always here for you," he said.

We went out and hit three or four times a week at the local baseball field. He never hesitated to pitch when I wanted to hit, but I didn't want to take advantage of his arm.

Before the end of the summer, Bo had to go back to juvie for a few months for failing his drug test for smoking weed. This time he would be in there for some months, and there was nothing my auntie could do about it. I was so disappointed, not so much in him, but because I knew he was the only one who was really there for me. It was our dream that I'd do it big in high school since he chose to dropout.

The chances of going pro from college are
less than 2% in basketball and football.

Chapter 5

Growing Pains

My mother sent Linda and me to Hamilton High School Music Academy in the fall of 1989.

She thought it would be a good way to explore our musical talents. My oldest sister went there too. It just made sense for all of us to be together in the same school, but the only hard part was that I didn't get to graduate with my friends who were still in junior high school. Nevertheless, I knew kids were getting drafted to the pros from high school, and I was determined to make that my story. Music was cool, but sports would be my way out of poverty.

Football season was in the fall, the beginning of the school year, and I couldn't wait to get to the coach's office and meet the head coach.

"My name is Sonny Weathers, and I want to play football this season, Coach," I said.

"You're kind of small to be playing football, ain't ya, kid?" said Coach Osborne, as I stood in his office, a young 14-year-old kid, 5'0 and 105 pounds wet.

"Yea, I'm small, but I'm tough," I responded.

He asked, "Have you ever played organized football before?"

"No, but I played tackle football in the streets, with my brother and his friends who were bigger than you," I replied.

Coach Osborne laughed and replied, "You're kind of spunky, kid. I like your confidence. How 'bout you come out and show us what you got after school?" he said.

"I'll be there," I replied.

The coaches were impressed with my athleticism and work ethics. After practice, I got fitted for my pads, however, I was so small they didn't have any that fit. The coach had to special order my own shoulder pads.

Against my mom's will, I signed up to play football. She thought I was in the marching band. My mom hated athletes; she would much rather me get a job than play sports.

"All black dudes just want to be jocks," she would assert. "I ain't raised you to be no jock. Besides you're too small for sports."

Though I was smaller than everyone on my football team, I had worked hard and earned myself a starting position at safety. Playing safety was like playing centerfield in baseball, which was going to make my transition in the upcoming baseball season easier.

The first half of my freshman year went pretty good. I'd gained a little popularity playing football, but I was really anticipating the beginning of my first high school baseball season.

* * *

When Bo was released from juvie in the beginning of December, he moved to Bellflower with his mother. I didn't get to see him much because he got himself a job, but we both looked forward to seeing one another during Christmas break.

As soon as school ended, I stayed with him for a week in Bellflower. It was obvious my brother had become institutionalized. He wore creased Dickies suits, Chuck Taylor's, brownies (gloves), and always had an ironed blue and black rag in his back pocket - he definitely had the look of a gangster.

We talked about how he survived in juvie, but he really didn't want to talk much about himself. He always managed to turn the conversation back on me. When he came back, he was almost 6'4" and here I was only 5'2." We looked like father and son next to each other. Though he had the persona of a grown man, a full goatee, a mustache, and hair on his chest, I knew deep down inside he was just a big kid.

"Bo, I hope you ain't ever going back to juvie. I need you out here."

Bo said, "I ain't bro, I promise this time I ain't going back. I'm going straight. From now on, I'm doing the right things. I'm working now. I want to help you out so you can have all your equipment for sports. You're a good kid, bro. You deserve the best."

Bo was one of the only people who said anything positive to me growing up. I felt confident with him around, like I could do anything.

That Christmas my whole family celebrated Bo being home. Against his will, he took a lot of pictures, which he hated. Bo also gave a speech before dinner, which was a first and something that showed his maturity.

"I'm glad to be able to spend Christmas with my family. I'm getting myself together and I promise that I am going to go on a different path and do right." Bo then bowed his head and led the prayer before dinner.

"Lord, I thank you for this auspicious occasion and a gathering of all my loved ones…"

I was proud. He prayed like a grown man, using big words.

I was all smiles while everybody else had their heads down.

* * *

Bo had to work the rest of the week, so we agreed to meet up the following Sunday. I couldn't wait to hang out. We had a lot of catching up to do. I couldn't wait to tell him about my high school experiences, but today was about him and the rest of the family just being together.

Two nights before New Year's Eve, I couldn't sleep. I was just up lying in bed for some strange reason. The phone rang around 2:30A.M., and out of nowhere, I heard my mom burst out a loud cry. I knew what that cry signified, and I immediately remembered this immense feeling of darkness and sadness take over my body. LaVassa and Linda started to scream as well. I stayed in the bed because I wasn't trying to hear any bad news at this point. I knew it was someone close. I was just praying that it wasn't Bo. Literally, seconds after that thought left my head, I heard my mother scream out, "BO, BO, BO!" I felt like I was in a horrible dream, waiting for someone to wake me. But I knew it was real once my sisters came in the room frantically telling me, "Get up! Get up! We got to go to the hospital. Bo's been shot!"

I was emotionless. I did not have any reaction. I was numb. I felt completely numb. I guess that was my way of dealing with what I knew was to come.

We rushed out the house and headed to Centinela Hospital in Inglewood. Bo was pronounced dead by the time we got there.

Everyone was crying, except me.

"I want to see him. I *need* to see him," I said as I pushed my way through all my family. My uncle offered to go with me, but I demanded to go alone.

As I walked into the cold, brightly lit room, he was lying on a gurney covered by a white sheet. I was overwhelmed by the feeling of pain, hurt, loss and disappointment. I could've never imagined this moment, but then again who could ever prepare themselves for a tragedy of this magnitude?

I pulled the sheet from over his face. The bullet holes were still fresh in his head, neck and chest. His closed eyelids were still moist from the tears that had fallen down his face. An image that has been engrained in my mind since that day. I don't know what happened to me in that moment. I had a feeling as if I was in a trance, having an out of body experience. I heard Bo's voice come over me, *"Don't cry, Bro."* The tears began rolling down my face. *"I'm still here. I'll always be with you. I'm counting on you to make it for the both of us. I'm just gone in the flesh."*

"How can I go on without you?" I cried.

"You know how. Be brave and stay focused on our plans. I love you," as his voice began to fade away.

The tears continued to flow down my cheeks. I had to pull myself together as I said my last goodbye with a kiss on his cheek. My best friend. My cousin. My brother was gone in the flesh. I felt a warming comfort over my soul because I knew that his spirit would always be with me. It was at this moment I knew the mission was greater than I was. I had a promise to fulfill and as long as I was living, I had to be the man of my family. As I shed my last tears, I turned around and walked out the door. I had to be strong for my mom and my family, so I cried no more.

My family was torn apart and in chaos in the waiting room. "It was a drive by," I heard his mom say with tears all over her face. Bo and his friend were in a car when the shooting took place. Bo shielded his friend's body from the bullets. His friend got shot once, and he was shot 13 times. My brother and his friend were victims of gang violence. I sat and listened, feeling hopeless, alone, sad, and angry all at the same time. Later, I talked to his friend who was also in the car. He told me, "Bo was my hero, and if it wasn't for him, I wouldn't even be here."

No one had to tell me that about my bro, nor did he have to take any bullets for anyone. If he loved you, I knew he would lay his life on the line. So, I wasn't surprised that my brother protected his friend. That was his character and one of the reasons I loved him so much. He was 100% true.

* * *

A week after Bo's funeral, school started. I had completely become an introvert. Replaying seeing Bo on the gurney under the white sheets tormented me. Looking back now, I think I was suffering from PTSD. It was something I never talked about with anyone. I never shared how hurt, sad, or alone I felt after Bo's death.

Whenever I began to think about him being gone or feeling sad, it would be for brief moments because I would remind myself I had to be strong to take care of my family. As a young man, I took on all the burdens of my family dysfunctions, pain from unexpected deaths of family members, generational poverty and a whole world of catastrophes that were beyond my young understanding - issues that were beyond my capability as a young man.

I was still in shock and did not even begin to grieve my brother's death. I finished out my freshman year and played my first season of baseball as we had planned. Considering everything that happened that school year, I did well in school and in baseball. I was 100% committed to the mission.

Looking back, I realize how traumatic the loss of my brother Bo was for me. Often times, I felt the feelings of being trapped and hopeless about how my life would turn out. Without any knowledge of what I was feeling, I was falling victim to inner city nihilism.

It was as if Bo had been haunted by street life, and with bleak opportunities for advancement, he succumbed to his environment. To 'make it out' of the streets is by no means an easy twelve-step program that people can follow. Everyone's story takes different turns; we all have unique paths. Eventually we must also learn to embody the strength, faith, and an imagination to change our circumstances.

The most difficult part of this process is actually starting it. How does someone who owns nothing on this land, or is undereducated, go about gaining access to the tools needed to improve his life? More importantly cultivating the tools needed to dramatically shift their lives? The thought alone has been enough to deter millions from even trying.

Yet, my strongest asset at this time was my imagination. As I stood ready to go to war with all things seen and unseen that stood in my way from 'making it.' Most importantly, I have to keep my promise to Bo.

Church – the place for spiritual beings

Chapter 6

A Family in Prayer

The death of my brother was still fresh in my consciousness, and I knew that church was the only place I would be able to ease the pain.

I wasn't the type to shout, speak in tongues, or praise the Lord in church, like my mom and sisters, but I believed wholeheartedly in the power of God. I made my joyful noise unto the Lord through music. Being a drummer was my way of getting out some of my pains and frustrations.

My mom used to make us go to church anytime she could - 3:30 Sunday service, Monday - Friday revival, Saturday choir rehearsal and back to church on Sunday. Often times we were in church seven days a week. The busy church life was not new to me because we were always very active in church. The pastor of our church was my mom's cousin, and our entire family worked together to help the church grow. Black churches were a place where families got together, and my family was no exception. You were able to learn ethics, morals and values.

Eventually I learned to put this high-church frequency into perspective. Our church had also moved to a much larger edifice in Long Beach and had grown from 60 members to over 300 members. The demand for my service as a drummer was also starting to pick up. I was beginning to play for many choirs and concerts in L.A. I was now making more money and was able to pitch in more with the bills. I was getting paid to play the drums, and getting paid helped keep peace in the house.

You would think that things would be better in my home since my dad was not living with us, but they really weren't. My mom was still angry with my sisters and me. I was now 15, and while she wasn't as physical, the verbal abuse was still a constant. It was obvious that my mom was completely miserable about how her life had ended up.

In hindsight, I now empathize with my mother's struggles and frustrations. She was a young thirty-something-year-old woman raising four children on her own, with an abusive and drug addict husband who came around sporadically. Church was her escape as well, as she would cling to her church mothers and sisters for support and prayer.

I remember, on our way to church there was a sign that read, "A family that prays together stays together." In the past, that sign held its significance in my life because no matter what or where my family was, we were still able to get together and pray.

Amidst all the drama and chaos, church was the place my entire family was able to find strength. But as the years went by, family members became too busy and consumed by the chaos and struggles in their lives, and church was no longer their rest haven.

Only about 65% of high school graduates enroll in college.

Chapter 7

Keeping My Promise

My dad came back to live with us my sophomore year in high school, a year I'd rather forget. The only good part about him being in the house was that he convinced my mom to let me play football. That didn't last long. However, I had to pick up the slack that my dad lacked, so I had to quit playing ball and play the drums more.

One thing I've learned over the years is that people rarely change. They can have every intention to do right, but the bottom line is that people are who they are. Not saying that God can't change a person because I know He can. It's just that when a person is on illegal drugs for instance, they can have every intent to do the right thing, but for that high, they'll steal, fight, and hurt the ones they love - and be sorry afterwards.

My dad was back to stealing my mom's car and pawning things in the house - typical behavior when he was not *himself*. It became a challenge to manage my grades. There were many sleepless nights, in addition to a hectic church schedule. As a result, my mom did not allow me to play baseball after football season.

My sophomore year flew by and my chances of getting into college on an athletic scholarship, let alone academic, became slim. I felt like the only way I could save my family was to make my dream a reality and play baseball. I had to do something quick.

The summer before my 11th grade year I finally started puberty and hit a growth spurt. My dad was in the house far less than the previous year. The days that he did spend in the house he would be in my mom's room asleep. It was like living in a house with a stranger that you could not trust around your things. We barely exchanged words when he did come around. I did not know him outside of all the drama and pain he caused my family, and at this point in life, I did not care to begin a relationship with him. I hated what he did to my family when he came around. I was embarrassed by his addictions and embarrassed that he was my father. I was becoming my own man and I was surviving without him.

* * *

I had grown six inches in the summer and was 5'10" the beginning of my junior year. It was like night and day with all the attention I received. I was the "new kid on the block." My twin sister, who previously referred to me as her 'nerd brother,' took me shopping to make sure I was going to make a stunning impact when I walked on campus with her. Not only had I grown taller, but I gained 30lbs of muscles from weightlifting.

Linda and I walked into school 10 minutes before the bell rang to make sure everyone was present for our grand entrance. Linda had her arm around mine to make sure everyone would notice me. She was the popular kid in school. Of course, I was nervous. I wasn't used to my new clothes and haircut.

"Who is this, Linda?" two of Linda's friends had walked over and asked.

"Oh, don't you remember my brother, Tiny, from last year?" she replied.

As I blushed at the flattery, I said, "I'm Sonny."

"Sonny, Sonny, Sonny...hmmm! I ain't seen you here before."

"I stayed low key," I said with a soft grin on my face.

Both of her friends grabbed me by my arm, and escorted me to class. "We're taking you to class, handsome."

I felt like a celebrity walking into class. My new look was an instant success. It felt great to get some attention. I tried not to let it get to my head, but I was quickly starting to like the new me.

My old grade school buddy, Bryan, who had attended Hamilton with me, had also noticed the new change and attention I was getting.

"Man, I'm glad the old Sonny is back," he said.

The previous year I had become anti-social, but no one really understood that I was still dealing with my brother's death. Something I still hadn't really gotten past. With all the new attention, I remained humble, but it was a little harder to stay on my mission. I didn't play football that fall, instead my new interest was running the streets and chasing girls. Still innocent, I started feeling the pressure of being the "last American virgin." It seemed like everyone was having sex but me. It wasn't like opportunities weren't there - I lived in a house with all sisters, and they had plenty of girlfriends - but I wanted my first time to be with the right girl.

A typical day at lunch before football practice, all the jocks and popular kids gathered around lunch benches. Most conversations entailed sex and who was getting some.

"You still ain't got none?" teased the captain of the football team who turned towards me.

Everyone laughed, but I was not the type to give into peer pressure.

"Naw," I said.

"Pretty boy scared of the love," one of the other players yelled while everyone else continued to laugh.

"Nah, I ain't scared," I replied. "I'm just not a slut like y'all. Y'all gonna mess around and get a disease or get someone pregnant. Besides I'd rather wait till I'm married."

"Married?" said the football captain. "When he gets him some, he gonna be whipped." All the other guys laughed.

"Nah, sex is supposed to be special," I replied.

"The only thing special is that end result," said one of the other jocks. Everybody laughed uncontrollably.

One of the most popular girls in school who was sitting at the table next to us said, "I think it's special he wants to wait until he's married, unlike you dawgs."

"Yep, and proud of it," said the team captain as he broke out into the dog bark. "Ruff, ruff!" he barked, as the others followed in laughter.

When I mentioned that my twin and I were gonna wait until we get married to have sex, things got a little serious.

One of the other players commented with a smirk on his face, "Linda a virgin? That's your sister? Yea, right!" While all the other players were in an uproar laughing, I didn't say a word. I just turned around punched him dead in his mouth, and a fight broke out. Luckily, the fight was broken up before the school officials got at us.

I couldn't wait to get home to confront Linda.

"I heard some of the football players was passing rumors that you been having sex with a couple of players on the football team," I said in a stern voice.

"They lying on me," she insisted.

I took her word for it and left it at that. I believed anything she said. Linda would never lie to me.

It seemed like everybody was having sex, even my best buddy, Bryan, from grade school. After school one day, he convinced me to go with him to a girl's house he was planning to have sex with. She promised him he would get to have sex with her if he brought me over for her friend. He told me his girlfriend's best friend's name was Keisha and that she had a crush on me. Against my better judgment, I went with him.

When we got there, the house was filled with smoke and there was a bottle of alcohol on the counter. His girl offered us a drink and asked if we smoked. Bryan didn't smoke, but he drank a little. Keisha laughed when I told her I didn't smoke or drink.

She said, "You must be one ah dem good boys." "No," I said. "It's just that I'm an athlete."

By this time my boy Bryan had gone into the back with his girl and left me and Keisha in the living room alone. Keisha immediately tried to go in for the kill. She turned on Jodeci's "Come and Talk to Me" to set the mood.

"Oh, this my new jam. Jodeci da bomb," she said." I replied, "Yea, they cool."

She started dancing seductively in front of me, as she started unbuttoning her shirt. "So, wassup Sonny Boy? I heard you was a virgin."

I didn't comment, I was hoping Bryan would come out the room so he could be my excuse for leaving. While I was sitting down, she stood between my legs as she continued unbuttoning her shirt and said "I didn't bring you here to talk, I wanna make out. You gonna let me get dat "D" or what?"

Keisha wasn't ugly or anything, but she wasn't the kind of girl I imagined losing my virginity to, although I was tempted. The fact that I knew she was high and had been drinking gave me the courage to stand my ground. The only thing I could think of to tell her at the time, "I have a girlfriend, Keisha."

"She go to Hamilton?" she asked. "No," I said.

"Well how she gonna know?" as she continued her advances.

"Keisha, you been drinking and you high. We can't do this," I said as she managed to straddle me on the couch.

But she insisted, "Sex is da bomb when you faded." "Keisha, I really don't think it's a good idea."

She jumped up and angrily yelled, "What, you scared ah dis?"

I didn't say a word. Luckily, Bryan had come out the room fixing his pants and asked, "What's goin' on in here? I heard some yelling," as if he was concerned about what was really going on.

"You brought this boy over here who scared to have sex," replied Keisha.

I looked over at Bryan and said, "Let's go."

We left. On the way home, I apologized to Bryan for rushing him. But he explained to me that he did not come out of the room because of what was going on, and that I was his

69

excuse to leave because he had ejaculated prematurely. We both laughed.

The next morning Keisha told everyone what happened and spread a rumor that I was gay. I didn't care. I had nothing to prove to anybody.

* * *

After a few months, I finally gave in to all the pressure to have sex. Her name was Leilani Moore. She was 26, tall, brown- skinned, with long silky hair. She was sexy, grown, and classy, unlike the girls that chased me at school. She was a woman – on top of that, she was a family friend. She treated me like a little brother, but deep down inside, she was my teenage crush. She was member of our church, and she sang in the choir. Every guy in the church wanted her, but for some reason, she always flirted with me. She gave me the kind of attention that I liked. She made me feel like a man, even though I was only 16.

Leilani would usually drop me and my sisters off at home after choir practice, but one night during my Christmas break, it was raining really bad, so we decided to just all spend the night at her condo. It wasn't the first time I spent the night at her place with my sisters, so that was nothing new.

On the way home, we were having a deep conversation about relationships, and since I was the only man in the car, everyone asked me for my two cents. Of course, I was always going to give the answer she wanted to hear.

"You're so sweet and kind. A true gentleman," she said as she stared at me in the rear-view mirror.

I just smiled.

"If you were older, you'd definitely be the kind of guy I'd be with."

Somehow, we locked eyes, and I could tell there was more to our glance.

Later that night after all my sisters had fallen asleep, it started pouring rain. Leilani and I went to her room to talk, as we often did. I don't know how we got to her showing me her new martial arts move. It just so happened that she slammed me to the bed, and we both fell on the floor with her on top of me. I thought I was in a movie...in slo-mo. My heart began to race, and our eyes caught each other's once again. We were now breath to breath, and it was a quick moment of awkwardness. Though I was so nervous, I reached up and kissed her. She pushed me off her angrily, and asked "Why did you do that?"

I jumped up and said, "I am sorry, Leilani. I didn't mean it."

She was lost between what was moral and what she felt in our kiss. She then said, "It was nice." At that moment, I grabbed her and then threw her on the bed. I'd seen enough movie scenes to know what to do. Here was my chance. I began kissing her, first on her mouth, then on her neck. She was now allowing me in, so I began unbuttoning her shirt and she tried to stop me one more time, but then gave into my seduction. She whispered in my ear, "Take me." We made love all night long.

I was spending most of my winter break with her. She took me shopping for new clothes, shoes, and anything I wanted. She spoiled me. When school started, she even gave me the keys to her car, and I didn't even have a license yet. When I pulled up to campus, I was dressed from head to toe in all my new gear and in a '91 Lexus. I was in a new world, and I loved all the new attention. My confidence was growing even more. I was a man now.

More than just the physical aspect of our friendship, she showed me the womanly love and attention I lacked at home. I felt like she cared about me and supported the things I wanted to do. I was young and vulnerable.

I played baseball even though my grades were not up to my mom's standards. I had finally made the varsity team. I didn't start, but I played a lot. Things couldn't have been any better for me and my social life. I was popular on campus and in the city now. And I was on my way to pursuing my dream of becoming a professional baseball player.

* * *

Out of nowhere a series of events happened that changed my whole world forever. One, my family left our church.

It was a typical Sunday afternoon in church. It was Family and Friends Day, so church was packed to capacity.

Everybody had been singing, praising, worshipping, and receiving the Word.

Out of nowhere, in the middle of the service, one of the missionaries walked to the front the church with tears flowing from her eyes and grabbed the mic as she normally did. This time her announcement wasn't the same.

"I've been having an affair with the pastor," she shouted.

Immediately, the deacons all rushed to grab her. There was chaos all over the edifice. Murmurs spread across the building and most people got up and walked out. My family was no exception.

Still devastated from Sunday's scandal, my mom came home early from work that Monday. Around this time, I had been skipping school to spend more time with Leilani. When I got home from practice, my mom asked me where I had been.

"I was at school," I replied.

"No, you wasn't. I went up to the school, and you weren't there. You're failing darn near all your classes, and I'm hearing you're playing baseball."

"I am not failing my classes," I said.

She said, "Yea, whatever! And who was you with today?" I stood there in silence.

"You were with Leilani? You been seeing her? Your sister told me that you been messing around with that older woman. I'm calling the cops right now."

I reached to grab the phone out of her hand.

My mom was not afraid to swing whatever she had in her hand at me, but at this point, I felt like I was too much of a man to be getting beat on. She picked up a broom stick and headed towards me.

"You ain't bout to hit me with that broom anymore," I told her.

"Oh, so you think you bad now? You think you grown? Because you having sex, and you got a little size on you, lil' punk?"

"No, mom. You just not going to be putting your hands on me anymore."

"Oh, what you going to do? Hit me like your daddy do?" she asked.

Tears rolled down my eyes, but I stood my ground and replied, "No mom, but you not going to be putting your hands on me anymore," I repeated.

"Then get out my house," she asserted.

I knew then there was no coming back from this. "Fine!" I grabbed my baseball cards and the clothes I had and left.

Desperate, with nowhere to go, I walked down the street to the pay phone and called Leilani. She told me that my mom had just called her and that I shouldn't call her anymore. That was the end of Leilani and me.

With my last quarter, I called my baseball teammate, Chris Cort. He came and got me, and I ended up staying at his house for the week without his parents knowing. But when his father caught wind of me staying, he told me I had to go.

The only other number I had was my summer league baseball coach and mentor to many youth in the inner city, Big Tone. My friend had dropped me off at his house in Windsor Hills. I begged him to let me stay with him and his mother, but he told me I had to get permission first from my parents. I did just that, and my dad happened to answer the phone.

He told me, "You're a big boy now. Do what you gotta do."

Deep down a small part of me wanted to hear him say, "*Come home, Son,*" because he was going to make everything okay. But he didn't, and I was officially on my own.

* * *

I did end my junior year fairly good that baseball season, but not enough to get any real attention. Considering how my life was going, my aspiration to be a professional baseball player seemed far away. I hadn't played organized baseball for any consistent periods in my life, I didn't have any support or motivation from my parents or family, and no one knew me as a baseball player. College now seemed farfetched because my grades were bad. I started to feel like all the odds were against me achieving my goal.

Because of all the rioting, violence and chaos in L.A. during this time, every emotion of fear I had was intensified. I never knew what I would face walking outside, and every day felt as though it could be my last. Would I fall victim to a drive by? Would I be harassed by the police because I fit some 'profile?' I was overwhelmed and consumed with so much doubt. I struggled mentally to keep everything I was dealing with into perspective and to focus on the one thing I had dreamed about since I was a child—baseball.

*　*　*

Living with Big Tone's family, I learned how to prioritize my life, and work towards my goals with a game plan. They provided all the necessities I needed to be successful. For the first time, I had my own room with a bed, three square meals a day, and a peaceful environment to focus. The only responsibility I had was to do well in school. Tone believed that the best path for me was to get an education, and sports was an opportunity to do so. But I saw school as an opportunity for me to make it to the big league, and that's where we differed.

I enrolled in summer school so that I could work on bringing up my grades before going into my senior year. I also worked hard to prepare for the SAT, which I knew nothing about up until that point. My senior year was all about working hard. I attended SAT prep classes every Saturday. I worked with tutors in school. When I wasn't studying, Tone and I worked in the batting cage.

The next goal was for me to make a name for myself in baseball. No colleges were knocking at my door, and maybe two scouts knew my name. Tone made sure that got a lot of playing time competing against all the inner cities top prospects, playing on the Saturday and Sunday adult leagues. For the first time in my life, I was playing baseball regularly. During the fall, I played in some scouting leagues against the area's top players. With a lot of work and dedication, I was beginning to make a name for myself.

By spring, I had mailed letters to all the colleges and top pro scouts inviting them to come check me out during my spring season.

* * *

"Weathers, come to my office. I gotta speak to you," said my baseball coach.

He was an old war vet and never really smiled much; I actually thought he didn't like me.

"What the heck you do this off season, kid? I got colleges and scouts calling me left and right about you!" he exclaimed.

I smiled and responded, "I been working hard, Coach."

"Well, I am making you the Captain of this team this year, and you better not disappoint me, or I'll have you on that bench quick," said the coach.

"Yes sir, Coach Kim. I won't disappoint you."

I couldn't have been any prouder of the progress and where my life was going. I was now prepared mentally to make my impact for my team and for Bo.

* * *

I opened the season with a ten-game hitting streak. For the first time, my baseball team was the news in the city, and I was the headline. I followed the momentum with seven homeruns in seven games, and I caught the attention from every Major-League scout in the area. I received scholarship offers from all the major colleges in Los Angeles as well.

That June, with an impressive .559 AVG, nine home runs, forty-five RBI's (runs batted in), I received All Metro-League Player of the Year honors. I made the *L.A Times* first team and California All American Honorable Mention, and I was Top 5 in every offensive category in the state. I also scored high enough on my SAT to qualify for a scholarship. I was on my way.

I never knew how it would happen, but it happened. I knew my brother would be proud of me for all the work I put in.

To top it off, I was selected in the 25th round by the Kansas City Royals that summer. Though I did not get drafted as high as I thought I should have, everything worked out the way it was supposed to. Bo's and my dream of becoming a professional baseball player had come true.

Less than 1% of high school students will play in the Major Leagues.

Chapter 8

Baseball Years –Part I

Big Tone, Linda, LaVassa, Cupcake, and my mother were at the airport to see me off that summer. I felt proud that I was able to fulfill my dream and the promise I made to my family. It was good to see them together again after all we had been through. I knew they were happy for me. My life had changed unbelievably in one year. Talk about hard work and dedication, I coined the terms. I couldn't have been prouder of myself, but with all the joy I was feeling, there was still more work to be done. My journey was now beginning, and I had no idea what to expect.

I had not flown on an airplane before, let alone gone out of the state. I figured it another act of bravery I had to overcome. My flight was headed to Ft. Myers, Florida home of the Kansas City Royals rookie minor league team.

I landed around 2:00P.M., and it was pouring rain; nonetheless, it was as humid as any typical summer day in Florida. When I got off the airplane, I was greeted by the Royals' General Manager at baggage claim. He drove me from the airport to the stadium where I formally checked into camp and was set up with all my gear and equipment. The field house was empty when I arrived.

"Everyone's back at the apartment. After you finish getting fitted for your gear, we'll head to the apartments so you can meet your roommates," said the GM.

We finished up and headed to my living quarters for the summer. They were luxury apartments located near Ft. Myers Beach. They were plush, nicer than anywhere I'd ever lived. They were fully furnished, and the only thing I had to get was my own bedding and toiletries.

I shared the three-bedroom apartment with three other ball players, Malcolm Cepedo, who was there living with his wife and child, Enrique Burgos, and Carlos Mendez, who were both from the Dominican Republic. All except Malcolm were from other countries and didn't speak English. Malcolm was from San Francisco, and he taught me the ropes while I was there. His father was a MLB Hall of Famer, so he knew a lot about baseball life on the road.

"Make sure you're up early for the buses to get to the stadium. If you're late, they'll leave you and you'll get fined," Malcolm said.

I made sure to set two alarms. I hardly slept that night from all the anticipation.

That morning I was the first one up and ready to go. The players met up in front of the apartment complex's main office. There were three vans there to pick us up. One van was filled with Latino players, another was filled with white players, and the third van, which I rode on, was mixed. I was not surprised to see the segregation. I figured that was how it would be.

I was quiet on my ride to the stadium. I guess there really wasn't much to say since I didn't know anybody.

When we arrived at the stadium that morning, the head coach, Bob Shaw, called me to his office.

"Hey, kid, we're going to sit you out a few games so you can get caught up on how things are run, and then we'll add you into the mix sooner or later."

"We got outfield drills for the outfielders in 20 minutes so make sure you're dressed and ready to go."

The Royals had drafted two other high school outfielders that summer who were much higher draft picks than I was. Their highest pick who was their 6th rounder, Gator Frazier, a talented athlete with phenomenal speed and athletic ability but fairly new to the sport. The other was Mo Smith, who was their 11th pick, and other than being big, there was nothing special about him. There were also three other outfielders there from the previous year trying to earn their shot. I already knew that getting a chance to play was going to be tough since I was the lowest pick of them all.

During the outfield drills, I must have showed up all the players because it seemed they did not care for me much afterwards. Even though I was a natural at some aspects of the game, I must admit I was raw because of my lack of baseball experience. Yet, my skills were promising.

After the drills, the outfield coach Chayo Tartabull, had taken a liking to me and teased the other players.

In his thick Latin accent, he said, "Hey, you guys got some competition out here!"

I took that as a compliment because he was the father of one of my favorite Big League ball players at that time, Danny Tartabull.

Everybody remembers their first at bat in the pros, and I could never forget mine. We were playing against the Minnesota Twins rookie club one afternoon. It had been two weeks into the season and I was beginning to get a little antsy sitting on the bench every day still hoping to get my shot. My first at bat was against a player, down from Double A, doing his rehab assignment. He had just struck out two of the previous batters with fastballs, in speeds I had never seen before. He had thrown in the mid to upper 90's and honestly, I was hoping the coach wasn't going to call me to pinch hit, but of course, he did.

"Weathers, grab a bat," he said. "Who me?" I replied.

"Yes sir. You're up," he said.

It was 1:30 in the afternoon, and it was at least 100 degrees. It was humid, and I was sweating bullets as if I had been playing all nine innings. I had to remain cool because this is what I had asked for. I took my warm up swings then went into the box. Honestly, everything was a blur. I was so nervous that my legs were shaking and cramping before I saw the first pitch.

"STRIIIIIIIIIKE ONE!" the umpire called. I just want to get this over with.

As the pitcher began going into his second windup, my legs began cramping emphatically which caused them to lock and led me to fall to my knees after the second pitch.

"STRIIIIIIIIIKE TWO!" the umpire called.

Within seconds of me falling, the umpire called time out so I could get my legs together. I could see everyone in both dugouts laughing hard. I was embarrassed.

"You okay, kid?" the umpire asked.

I took a deep breath. At that point, I just wanted to head to the showers.

The next pitch came. I couldn't tell you if it was a ball or a strike, but I swung as hard as I could.

"STRIKE THREE! YOU'RE OUT!"

And the ball game was over.

It's tough for any player to come off the bench, as a pinch hitter, because frequency is what enables players to get into their rhythm. I didn't understand that at the time and ended up putting unnecessary pressure on myself to do well that season, and instead I ended up having an awful year. I knew then that I was up for a great challenge trying to make it to the big leagues.

I received the inspiration I needed from Bob Shaw, our head coach. He was a good man, a devoted Christian and never hesitated to share the word of God with those who were willing to listen. He held Bible studies regularly during the week for those in need of spiritual guidance.

He used to say to me, "Keep your nose clean, kid."

I interpreted that as his way of telling me not to get into any trouble. With all the outfielders on the Royals roster, it was clear they wouldn't hesitate to send players home who couldn't get their acts together, so I did my best to stay in Coach Shaw's good graces. I would imagine it being tough to be a Rookie league coach, having to deal with a bunch of hot head kids, but Coach Shaw was perfect for the job. I learned a great deal from him about life and being a man of God in sports.

He used to say, "If it's God's will for you to make it to the big leagues, you've already made it." Those words of wisdom guided me in more aspects than just sports.

Some good did come out of that season. I developed what I thought would be a lifelong friendship with the Twins first rounder, Torii Hunter, who was a friend of Gator Frazier. All three of us hung out a lot off the field. We shared facilities with the Twins, so we were around each other often. Being that there were few African-Americans on both teams, we all hung tight, but the three of us more than most.

I had such a horrible season, and if I hadn't been for Torri and Gator, I would've felt so out of place in Florida. However, I couldn't wait to get back home and see my family and friends in L.A.

* * *

I had received my signing bonus for $25,000, more money than I had ever seen. I left Tone's house and got an apartment for myself on the Westside and was happy to be in my own space. I wanted to buy everything I always wanted, but the first thing I did was make due on a promise to my mother as a kid - I bought her a pair of diamond earrings.

They were wrapped in gold and silver. A pair of one-carat diamond earrings. I told her there would be more to come, and she smiled from ear to ear. It was another rare moment to see her smile, and I'd do anything to keep that smile on her face. For all that she'd been through, I just wanted to see her happy.

"Just like I promised," I said.

"They're so beautiful!" she said as she took the earrings she had in her ear out and replaced them with the new diamond earrings.

I also wrote her a blank check that she used to get all the appliances she needed for her apartment.

I didn't think twice about spending because I felt there would be much more to come. On top of my apartment, I also bought my first car, a used Honda, and I spent lavishly on my family and friends.

I took a trip to Pine Bluff, Arkansas to see my baseball buddy Torii. Traveling to Arkansas changed me because I got a chance to witness something special which I lacked, brotherhood. Even though evidence of poverty was more blatant in Pine Bluff than Los Angeles, there was still a strong sense of community and brotherhood amongst the people. Anyone who made it out of Pine Bluff had the support of the entire city. The love was so real, I honestly didn't want to leave. It was like one big family there.

During my time there, Torii and I prepared hard for the upcoming spring training. We lifted weights, ran, and played as many pickup games as we could. I was destined to come back in top condition. I was glad for the opportunity to spend my offseason with Torii. He was very competitive, which I liked, and it pushed me to excel in my game.

I gained my confidence back, and I felt like this was going to be my breakthrough year. I was competing with Double A and Triple A prospects who I did well against, and I was sure I could possibly make my move through the Royals organization and become a prospect.

Baseball Years Part II (On the Road)

Spring training had rolled around, and the Royals sent me back to the Rookie League. Though I was disappointed, I didn't worry too much because at the very least, I knew I could make the short-season A-team. I was excited about the possibilities, and being at my first spring training meant I was going to meet all the Royals prospects and Big Leaguers I had read about. We stayed in beautiful dormitories in Haines City, Florida, which was a half-hour outside Orlando.

It wasn't long before I had become a hot name that spring. My talent and growth had made such an impression on the Royals that all the coaches and staff knew my name. I had outshined all the outfield prospects that were signed that year, hitting over .400 in spring training. But to my dismay, the Royals kept me with the extended spring team, and I headed back to Ft. Myers. Of course, I was disappointed.

There were six outfielders again competing to make the Short-Season A-squad, and because the players last year were drafted much higher than I was, they were the Royals' priority. But I was on a mission. I finished out extended spring hitting above .300, and I had even made captain of the team.

To my dismay again, after extended spring camp broke, Coach Shaw told me that they were going to keep me in Rookie ball one more season but reassured me that I was a prospect and they were impressed by my improvement. I knew deep inside the Royals knew I could play the game. I just had to be patient once again and wait for my chance to do my thing. After all, I was only 19 and still had a lot of maturing to do physically.

The season began, and the Royals had finally promoted me to hitting third in the lineup. Even though I got off to a slow start, I was seeing and hitting the ball hard. I knew this was going to be my year. The team was loaded with talent, and our goal was to win the Gulf Coast championships.

Things were looking bright. After 20 games, we were 18-2.

Things couldn't have been going any better for me.

* * *

Then one cloudy afternoon during late innings, the bases were loaded with the winning run on third. We had two outs. I was up to bat and already had two strikes. The next pitch was a curveball that I bounced slowly to shortstop. I knew the only play he had was to first. I ran as fast as I could and slid feet first into first base. I was safe, but it was the end of my season. I fractured my ankle in two spots, my tibia and fibula.

I didn't remember much of what had happened after the play. The only thing I remember is waking in the hospital. The players said I had passed out.

I felt like my whole world had just come to an end. My career that was finally beginning to come together had taken a hard turn, and I was falling apart mentally. The feelings of hopelessness and anger began to resurface, and I felt like I did not have anyone who would understand how I felt. If baseball was not going to work, then I would have broken my promise to Bo.

During this time, I thought about my brother so much. I knew that if he was still around, he would be the person I could talk to, and he would always encourage me to keep at it. I had so many questions and had become so angry with life and God. I felt like He was punishing me when I fractured my ankle. *How could He punish me like this? I wasn't a bad person. I treated everyone with respect. I didn't lie or cheat anyone. Why me? My family was counting on me. What was I going to do now?*

* * *

I returned back to L.A. that summer to start my rehab at the Kerlan-Jobe Clinic. I got most of my support and encouragement from the other professional athletes doing their rehab. I had become withdrawn from my family because I only heard from them when they needed money; and the pressure to support their needs without having anyone there for me was overwhelming. My new lifestyle already had me feeling alone inside, but after the injury, this only intensified.

I began hanging with some older guys from my neighborhood. I had grown up with most of the OGs since I was in elementary school, and most knew me for my fighting prowess and my no-nonsense attitude. I was hot-tempered and always ready for a rumble, and if you disrespected anyone I was with, there would be problems. I was known for fighting in the clubs and representing the hood. If it weren't for sports, there is no doubt in my mind that I would have been drawn more into the street life because, other than baseball, that's where I found refuge. But most of my peers kept me away from going too deep into the street world. They would always suggest I stay training for baseball and stay out of trouble. They probably figured me to be a well-to-do kid who was just acting out. Little did they know about my upbringing and the pain in my heart. I was more like a ticking time bomb.

After the fun wore off I got back into preparation for baseball. I trained just as hard as the previous year, but this time I was much stronger and faster from all the training done in rehab. I went back to spring training, and the Royals had sent me back to extended spring camp. I figured they did not know what to expect from me, but to add insult to injury, the Royals had drafted two high school first round draft picks in '94, Carlos Beltron and Juan Lebran. Now, the Royals shifted their concentration to their first-round picks, and I felt like they had pretty much forgotten about me. Since I was such a low draft pick, I didn't have an agent to lobby on my behalf, and my dreams of making it to the pros began to dwindle.

I didn't have anything else to fall back on because I had only planned my future around being a professional baseball player. The money from my signing bonus was practically gone. I did not have anywhere to live in Los Angeles because I had given up my apartment months earlier because of all the traveling I was doing. The only guarantee I had was my scholarship money the Royals gave me in my contract.

It was 1995 and talk about releasing me was beginning to loom around management. I was basically told that if I didn't get myself together this season, the Royals were going to send me home.

I was 20 years old and back to extended spring for a second season. Luckily, I ended up being promoted to short season A-ball. That's where pro teams send their top draft picks or college picks to get their first taste of the minor league life. I was happy I finally got out of rookie ball and I could begin my career. The Royals farm team, short season A-ball club was in Spokane, Washington that year, and Al Pedriguez was the coach. This was what I had been waiting for all my life, minor league baseball life.

We stayed in the dorms at Gonzaga University that year, but players were housed in a private area away from the students to make sure we stayed focused. Spokane was a quiet town with very little to do, which was fine by me because I could eat and sleep baseball. I could stay grounded.

In addition to a couple college picks that year, the Royals had sent three outfielders to Spokane from extended spring. I was the most talented of the outfielders, so I was sure I would get my time to shine.

The Indians was the name of our team and we wore white
and blue pin stripes with the red letter on the front. The facility/organization was top notch. It was a 100% improvement from Rookie ball. The Indians held Media Day for us, and the reception from the fans was awesome. The fans gave me the name "Machine Gun" for my good throwing arm and because I was from L.A.

I felt like things were starting to look up again. The first two weeks I was in the top ten in batting averages. I even moved up in the lineup to fifth, which was a huge promotion. But then things began to change. I began to see less and less playing time on the field as they had to let other player have opportunities.

I tried going to the coach's office and asking why I wasn't playing anymore, and he explained that the Royals were trying to evaluate their prospects. To me that meant that I was no longer one of them. I did not understand that organizations put players through different tests to see how well they handled adversity. It was the business part of the game, and I was too immature to understand it at the time. Instead I began to worry and stress about my future and not making it to the 'Bigs.'

The 'at bats' became more and more infrequent. I was getting one at bat a game, and I was not looking good. My average was going down and so was my confidence. So, I decided to take my life in my own hands. I decided to quit.

I called my grandmother CJ in Los Angeles and told her I was coming home. I explained the situation and expressed that I needed to take control of my life. I told her that the Royals owed me $80,000 in school money and that I wanted to go to college and pursue an education.

I went behind the Royals' back and scheduled a flight home after returning home from our road trip. I had even called a local junior college in L.A. to find out about playing football during the upcoming season. The only person I told was my roommate, Gator Frazier, who said he wanted to do the same. I had already taken the SAT and had the grades to get into a junior college. I wanted to play football at a JC and then transfer to a Division I university after one season. My only setback was that I did not have much experience playing football, with the exception of when I played in the streets growing up and my limited time in high school. I was going to take my chances and beat the odds. I had made my mind up, and I was going to leave my first love, baseball.

Less than 1% of high school seniors will be drafted by an NFL team.

Chapter 9

Prime Time - Part I

At the end of the summer, I moved back to L.A. to live with my grandparents. They had converted an apartment to a senior facility, and I had to work the family business as a part of the agreement to live with them. There was no turning back. I had to make the most of this move. It would actually work for both of us. I figured my grandmother needed a stable man around. Even though she had my dad, he was still on drugs, so she never could count on him.

It was never a dull moment at my grandmother's house. Not only did she run a business single-handedly, but she kept a beautiful home, cooked breakfast, lunch and dinner every day, washed our laundry, and encouraged and motivated everyone around her. She loved her family and did whatever she could to keep the family close. Even with so much going on in the house, at the end of the day, it was a family and everyone loved and supported one another. It was a different experience than what I was used to during my childhood. She made it easy for me to focus, and I had plenty to do.

I registered for classes at West L.A. for the fall semester and met with the football coach. He heard about me and my accomplishments in high school, so he was excited to have me be a part of the team.

"Sonny Weathers," said Coach Holmes. "How might I help you?"

"I wanna play football, Coach," I said.

"What about baseball? I've been following your career. We're always proud when someone from the city makes it," he replied.

"Well, I wanna play football too, Coach. I think I'll make a good wide receiver and possibly get a scholarship. I wanna play two sports and be the next two sports star," I said.

"We can use all the help we can get this season," said Coach. "It'd be good to have a pro athlete around. I'll see you at practice!"

West L.A. had a lot of really good athletes on the team. I was amazed how talented most of these guys were, but most were just misguided. They weren't serious in my opinion with all the drinking and smoking they were doing. Most of them showed up to practice high. But since they all had much more football experience and knowledge than I had, I sat back and learned from them.

I played wide receiver, the starting kick returner, and special teams that season. My goal was to play one season and get enough film to transfer to a university. I had a long way to go, but I knew it was possible. West L.A. was known for putting big names into colleges. The year before me, Keyshawn Johnson had just left, played one year and went to USC. So, I was willing to take my chances. I actually got a chance to meet him, and he was very insightful and inspired me to keep pushing. I heard a lot about his journey and what he had endured growing up in L.A. He told me to handle school and professional sports like businesses. Funny enough, he carried a briefcase when he came to the college to get some of his final paperwork. I liked that. It showed me something. I took his advice and carried myself as if I was a businessman and didn't get caught up with drama at West L.A. College.

Even with all the talent we had at West L.A that season, we didn't win very many games. It's not easy to get recruited when you're not from a winning program. I also didn't get much playing time at wide receiver, and when I did play, I didn't get many balls thrown my way. I did have a couple of nice runs as a kick returner, but I learned that practice speed and game speed are two different worlds.

Most of the time I used to be out there lost on the field. Every athlete feels like they should play or start, but when they get on the field, they often look like idiots when the ball comes to them, especially if they drop the ball. Or if they do catch it, everything is so fast, it's hard to see. The coaches know this. They watch practice film. That's why they're coaches.

I was taught a major lesson in football. Whatever you do on the field, you do it full speed, and that I did. It was the reason halfway through the season, the coach moved me to defense back. He felt I had a future as a DB, so he moved me to free safety. He also thought it would be a perfect position for me because of my background in baseball as an outfielder and my aggressive nature. He believed I had what it took to be a Division I talent. At this point, I didn't argue about the move. I needed film, so I did whatever the coach asked.

The season was coming to an end, and I wasn't getting the kind of attention I expected, nor did I put up any significant numbers to make any difference. The coach had plans for me to be his starting DB for next season, but I had my own plans and obligations to my grandma I had to fulfill. She told me I had to be gone by January because they were moving my grandfather's mother into my room. Stress was starting to hit me - the fear of being homeless again and not knowing my next move was looking me right in the face.

I decided to call the Royals and asked them to take me back, and they did. I now had somewhere to go when the semester was finished.

I told my grandmother the Royals had accepted me back, so she made arrangements for me to stay there until spring training began. I was already in great shape from playing football, but what I needed now was to get back into baseball shape. I stayed in the batting cages and played in the adult Saturday and Sunday leagues to prepare.

To keep myself occupied until spring training in March, I enrolled in some physical education and general education classes at Pierce Junior College, which in hindsight was the best thing I could've done. Enrolling in classes that spring would enable me to play football that upcoming fall.

When I went to camp with the Royals that spring, I was assigned to the A-ball squad. I knew it would be a challenge making the team. Not only was I up against old players, but now all of the Royals attention shifted to their two first round draft picks, Carlos Beltran and Juan Lebran. If I didn't make the squad, I would be sent back to extended spring for a 3rd time. I could not afford to go back to rookie ball because now I had a baby on the way back home.

I had a decent spring training. I batted over .300 and hit a couple of home runs. Word in camp was that the Royals were going to let me go after spring training. It was a numbers game, and three weeks later, I was cut from the team. The Royals owed me scholarship money in my contract, so I went back to Pierce College and made up the classes I missed during spring training. I decided to play football that fall at Pierce to try to earn a scholarship to a Division I.

When I got to Pierce, the first thing I did was meet with head coach, Bill Norton. Coach Norton was a stern, no nonsense man who was bluntly honest. A lot of the players did not like him, but he was a man of integrity, so I had to respect him.

After our meeting, Coach Norton took me on a tour to see more of the facility when a sky-blue Cutlass on Dayton wheels, playing loud music pulled into the parking lot.

"There he goes now," said Coach Norton. "The player I was telling you about, our All-American Scoop Brooks."

"Hey Mr. Brooks, I would like you to meet a new member of our team, Mr. Sonny Weathers."

He walked up to me with that gangster swag and said, "Weathers? I know that last name. Cuzz, you any relations to Karl Weathers? You look like cuzz."

I laughed and replied, "Yeah, he was my uncle." "Was?"

"Yea, Karl died," I said.

"Ahh, I did not know dat. Cuzz, you don't remember me, I'm Scoop, Karl's stepson," he said.

After thinking about it for a few seconds, I realized I did remember who he was and that we used to hang out when we were kids when I lived in Carson. We used to get into mischief together. I remembered he was wild when we were kids, but we were always cool.

"What a small world!" he exclaimed as we embraced like long lost brothers.

I learned a lot from Scoop, as he wished to be called. Though we were the same age, he taught me a lot about street life. He grew up fast, spent time in and out of correction facilities, and ran the Valley. He introduced me to everyone as his family and treated me like it. We trained a lot that off season, and I credit him for my football knowledge.

The season had rolled around and I was starting as running- back and spent half the time as wide-receiver. We played in the same conference as West L.A., so I had an opportunity to play against my old coaches and teammates. The fact that I had never played running back in my life except in practice, let alone caught a pass in a college or high school game, was in the back of my head. The only thing that mattered to me was success.

That fall at Pierce College I had gained a lot of notoriety and respect from the players and my peers for all my hard work and discipline. That season I earned decent numbers on offense and received All Western State Conference Honorable Mention Honors in '95. I managed to become a hot recruit because of my versatility. To add to a successful season, I had a brand new baby girl born on Thanksgiving Day.

I had received many letters and scholarship offers from Division I teams. I chose Bowling Green.

Prime Time - Part II

I went to summer camp at Bowling Green in '97 to train. The goal was for me to play running back, so I had to pick up weight. I gained 10 pounds of muscle, and I was walking around at 210lbs and stronger than ever. I couldn't wait to experience college life and play Division I football. I was ready for A Different World - no pun intended.

My family was happy that I had made it back on top once again. I worked really hard in the classroom to make it this far. I was able to manage and make the grades to make a successful transfer. Now I had grown accustomed to figuring out life on my own. I had to keep pressing forward. I had a child now, so I had big responsibilities to consider.

Life in L.A. was never going to change. My peers and family were still trying to find their own identities, and I guess it appeared I had found mine in sports. Everyone knew me as an athlete, but deep down inside I was probably as unsure about my future as anyone else.

Bowling Green was a new opportunity and my last chance to make it as a professional athlete to earn enough money to support my family. Having a successful football career in college meant I could possibly make it to the NFL or get the chance to make it to MLB Rule 5 Draft and get another shot at playing professional baseball. I still believed I had what it took to make it as a professional athlete. After all, playing sports was all I felt I could do to support my family the way I wanted.

I played a little at running back in 1997, but I started at kick-return. I was one of the fastest runners on the team. I also played on all the special teams. I didn't mind because I loved contact, and I wanted to be on the field as much as I could. I always found it weird that players used to get upset when the coaches put them on Special Team, but I looked at it as an opportunity to play anywhere and in all phases of the game. I embraced all my opportunities to play, and it was probably why I was treated favorably by all the coaches. I felt like I was too grown of man to get hollered at, so I made sure I did what I had to do to handle my business.

Our first game that year was against Louisiana Tech, and I started at kick-return (KR). I was nervous, but I had worked really hard that off season and at fall camp, so I was ready. The very first kick I returned for 40 yards, and it was on from there. I had another return for 50 yards that was called back for a holding penalty and I carried the ball a few times but nothing big. We lost that game, but my KR abilities got me a little media attention. This was different from JC football, because my performance, as small as it was, got some attention from the news and the local papers. It wasn't enough though. My goal was to get to the NFL. I wasn't only trying to be a college star.

The next game we played against Ohio State. They had a few All-Americans on their team and a linebacker who was projected to be the #1 pick in the up and coming draft. I started RB on our first possession. My first carry was for 5 yards, a hard stretch play up the middle. Even though it wasn't for many yards, I ran over that LB, and I was on top of the world. I came to play and show the world I could compete with the top players in the country. I got a lot of recognition for my play once again; I had over 100 yards in total offense that game.

During the middle of the season our defensive back coach called me to his office and asked if I would mind switching to cornerback. I had never played that position before, but like all of the other positions, I knew I would have to learn overnight. I told the coaches that it would be challenging for me to learn all our defensive schemes and asked if they would mind if I just played man to man all game. They just about jumped out their chairs, "Heck yea, kid!" they exclaimed with excitement.

Lining up man-to-man was intimidating for many players, but, it reminded me of when I was younger and used to play football in the streets with my brother and my friends. I finished the rest of the season playing both ways defense and offense. There were only a few players in college that year that played both ways, so I was sure I was making my case as an NFL prospect.

I ended the season with a few highlights, one of the biggest in my first game. I started at cornerback, and I made Player of the Game. I also set a new school record for the longest kick-return and received a plaque from AT&T for the "Long Distance Play of the Day." Bowling Green also awarded me with the Special Teams MVP plaque and allowed me the opportunity to make myself an NFL prospect. But I knew I still had a lot of work to do to get prepared for the next season.

* * *

Immediately after the season was over and with all my financial aid money saved, I went home to see my daughter. I bought her everything for Christmas. I never hesitated to give her anything she wanted. I wasn't around much because of my sports career, but any chance I could spend with her, I was there. I didn't spend too much time visiting my family during winter break either, but we did get together on Christmas Day, and it felt good to have all my siblings around at the same time. I usually stayed away from my extended family because there was so much drama, and I needed the peace.

That spring the pressure was getting to me to be the best athlete I could be. The NFL Scouting Day was coming up at the end of spring to evaluate and rate the top seniors for the next year. With so much on my shoulders, I had to make sure I was going to give myself every opportunity to succeed.

The head coach called me to his office to tell me how pleased he was with the commitment I made to Bowling Green and if I would mind switching to wide receiver. He thought I would be able to add some fire power to the offense with my speed and knowledge of the offense, so I gladly accepted.

Early that spring, management caught wind that there were a few players on my team that were using steroids, and I was soon confronted about the issue. I had never cheated and had been posed with the same situation while playing baseball, but the pressure I felt playing football was more intense. This time it was different. I knew it was my only chance to get back to grace in sports. I had to make it. I was homeless when I was not in school, and I now had a daughter to support. I was desperate to make it to the NFL and was willing to do anything to do so.

I began using steroids during that offseason to enhance my athletic capabilities, and it was the worst decision I had ever made. I had lost 20lbs of fat and I was ripped up benching over 400lbs and squatting over 600lbs. I was also running my forty-yard dash in 4.4 seconds, which was NFL caliber. I am sure everyone noticed my vast physical emergence. I was known to be a disciplined hard worker in the weight room before, but I had become leaner and much more explosive.

Spring Ball came around and I had developed into a NFL prototype athlete in just three months. When confronted by the head coach about my involvement with steroid usage, I lied even though he knew otherwise. My participation in the events landed me in the dog house with all the coaches. My integrity as a player now meant nothing to anyone.

I went home that spring break and all my friends had noticed my physical transformation. I didn't tell anyone I used steroids, but they were all excited about the possibility of me going to the pros. On the outside, I appeared to have it all together once again, but internally I felt ashamed because I cheated, and the possibility of not making it again loomed over me.

I returned to school after the break and continued my training. I anticipated going home for the summer to train with area top college prospects and NFL players in L.A. Summer came around, and I got my chance to work with one of sport's top conditioning trainers.

When I began school in the fall, I realized I would not qualify for graduation for the upcoming spring, but would graduate the following fall. That was a big blow mentally because I thought I would be done by the next summer. I was stressed to the max my senior season, and I knew trying to get to the NFL was going to be tough with all the negative issues surrounding my life. Coaches were aware of my dysfunctional upbringing and life back in L.A. and the fact that I was a young father. I was turning 23 years old, playing at a small unranked college, and I didn't have any consistent experience at any particular position I played. Between the guilt of my steroid usage and an injury from baseball, I knew something would surface when an NFL team did their investigation on me. I felt I had the world on my shoulders, and I was ashamed of my personal life.

I didn't have any male mentors I could talk to, ones who didn't have any vested interest in my involvements with football. My stresses escalated into the preseason camp and later into the early season. To add insult to injury, my position coach and I weren't seeing eye-to-eye. I had lost my confidence and their trust because of my steroid usage, and I was frustrated because I could not control or change anything I had done.

BG had decided to build on their future by playing their true freshmen over me. For the first two games of the season, I was supposed to be their go-to man, but I only got one ball thrown to me during the two games.

Our second game during the 1998 season, we played against Penn State. I got one carry at RB for 14 yards and one pass thrown my way in the fourth quarter. I felt like my chances were vastly fading, and to make matters worse, I had suffered a hip injury in our first game that I didn't tell the coaches about, and it worsened after the Penn State game.

That following Monday, before practice, the head coach called me into his office.

"Weathers, your name has been coming up quite a bit in this office. I hear you have something you want to talk to me about," said the coach.

"Yeah, Coach. I just wanted to know why I haven't been getting much playing time these last two games," I responded.

He said, "Well, son, there's been a lot of speculation about steroid use, and we want to quiet things down before putting you back in the limelight. And what is this I hear about you being injured?"

"I want to give you 100%, but I injured my hip at the end of the last game, Coach. I didn't have any stats these last two games, and now I'm hurt. With all that's going on, why not just red shirt me?" I asked.

"That's out of the question. Besides, I need you here to help me build up the younger guys," he said.

The phone rang. "Let me take this call. We'll talk after practice," he said.

Later that day, I went to practice, and my position coach was upset that I missed rehab, but he didn't know I'd had a meeting with the head coach. I wanted to know why I wasn't getting any playing time. I felt like my life was literally spinning out of my control.

"Missing rehab in unacceptable," said my position coach. "You're going to be sitting on the bench this next game," he said jokingly while the other players laughed.

Heated words were exchanged, and I walked off the field. I had quit and wasn't going back.

* * *

Once again, the head coach called me to his office and told me he wanted me to come back. The last thing I ever wanted to do was be at odds with my coaches. I had really grown to love my teammates and BG with all my heart. It wasn't easy walking away from football. I gave my all to the program. But I was losing myself and found it hard to focus.

To make matters worse, I dropped out of school that semester with nowhere to go. No one in my family knew I quit football. I needed to get away and sort things out for my sanity. It seemed like nothing I was doing was working out for me. Truth is I didn't love football. I played because I felt I had to. I was in search of something far greater than fame and fortune. I was in need of internal peace but did not know where to find it.

* * *

Returning home, I had to accept that peace wasn't there either. When I got back to L.A., I stayed wherever I could and pretty much lived out of my suitcases.

I got in contact with an agent who felt I had enough film to get me a workout with some Arena squads and maybe some NFL teams. I had to do something. My goal was not to play any arena football or anything less than the NFL, but the arena leagues paid a grand a month and I needed the money. He told me about a new 8-team league called RFL (Regional Football League) that was composed of ex-NFL players and college players. They were paying at the least 30 Grand for a three-month season that started in April. In the meantime, he got me a workout with a few arena teams in hopes to earn money and to keep getting playing experience.

I returned home and was feeling desperate. My daughter's mom was raising her alone, and my financial contributions were becoming an issue. My resources were running thin, so I decided to register at BG with no intentions of returning. I got my financial aid check and loan money. I was a hustler at heart. I was able to help my daughter's mom a little because I knew her patience was growing thin with me for not helping out. April rolled around, and it was time to leave.

I flew to Ohio to attend the training camp for the RFL, Regional Football League, in April. Of course, I made the team. I signed a $35,000 contract and immediately signed a lease for an apartment.

To my surprise, the league ended up folding before the first game, and no one was paid. I was stuck with an apartment and no money.

I was 24 years old, a college dropout, soon-to-be homeless, and with a child to support. I had no work experience and nowhere or no one to turn to. My grandmother was the only one who offered me a place to stay, but again, it was conditional. I had to take care of the seniors at her center.

Most boxers start fighting between the ages of 8-10.

Chapter 10

The Stage

By the time I was 25 years old, I knew it was time to hang up the cleats. It became increasingly difficult for my agent to get me contracts to play Arena Football, and by now I had already accepted that my chances of having a career in the NFL or MLB were nonexistent. Nevertheless, it was not an easy decision for me to leave the world of football behind because I had allowed it to become a major part of my identity - who I thought I was. The quest to discover who I was as a person and as a man had begun to magnify at this point because I could no longer masquerade as the 'talented athlete' I once was. I had a child and a family that depended on me to be there emotionally, physically and to provide; and this was something I struggled with greatly. Not to mention my own internal conflicts and burdens of being considered a failure to my family.

Somewhere along the way I took on the burden of rewriting my 'mistake' of walking away from baseball and so many other 'bad choices' I made. I didn't understand at this point that there really are no mistakes in life, but only lessons learned. I wanted to prove to everyone that I had what it took to be successful and prosperous.

The immense pressure I felt to be the man in my family that everyone could be proud of and look up to remained at the forefront of many of the decisions I made. Yet again, I did not waste a second to evaluate anything I had done and gone through in life. Looking back was too painful to even acknowledge so I quickly moved on to the next thing.

The summer was approaching, and I had to try something new. I had to find a way to get money, so I got a job stocking groceries at the local grocery store. Of course, I had become the laughing stock of all my peers, but I really didn't let it bother me too much because I knew it was temporary.

I needed that job so I could save money for a car and a down payment for an apartment. I was only making $8.50 an hour, so I knew it would take more time than I had to get back on my feet. Luckily, I got paid every Friday, and I was able to save the little money I earned. I guess a slow nickel beats a fast dime this time.

In a matter of three months, I was able to save up enough to get an apartment, but then I was laid off. I could never catch a break. I was a God-fearing man and I wanted better than to become a hustler or to work at trivial jobs, but my faith and confidence in myself to do much else was weary at this time. I had only envisioned myself as being an athlete, and now that I had to rebuild my life doing something else, I didn't know where to begin.

Just when I thought I had run out of choices, a simple phone conversation with my older sister, LaVassa, sparked a new interest. She suggested that I try my hand in acting.

"Well, I invited you over today because you been on my mind and I've been praying for you lately. I know over the last few years, we haven't communicated much, and I know our upbringing was hard, but, I really want to help you get your life together. That starts with getting your relationship with God on track, so you really need to get right with God."

I always looked up to LaVassa. She was my big sister. It was hard to take advice from a girl, but, just knowing that she cared was what I needed and had been searching for.

"You were always funny and had a great sense of humor as a youngster. You're handsome and very charismatic. I'm working in Hollywood now, and I think you should try your luck in the Industry. I got your back. You know cousin Holly is in the business as well, and we can help you. You just gotta put in the work which I believe in my heart you will do. I really think you should try acting."

Unless I was playing sports, the truth was, I was nervous about being on stage in front of cameras. But I figured, at that point, I had more to gain than to lose. After all, I needed to do something that would make me some big money, so I took her advice.

She connected me to a casting agency that sent me out on auditions for the shows that she worked on as an assistant casting director. Of course, it wasn't going to be easy trying to get in the acting world, but I had LaVassa and my cousin, Holly, who managed a few big clients during this time. I never wanted to ask my family for help because I wanted to make it in life on my own accolades just as they had.

However, one of the best ways to become successful is to learn to use the resources you have access to right then and there.

I was feeling hopeful about my future again, and decided to enroll in junior college full time in Fall 2000 so I could complete the requirement for my associate's degree. I found weekend employment working at a group home. I went to school and auditions during the day and acting classes in the evenings. I kept myself busy and focused that year.

Acting wasn't what I imagined I would be doing, but I was all in. By the time pilot season rolled around that spring, LaVassa had gotten married and her career was doing well. She promised me that she would do all she could to look out for me in the game. She told me that Holly managed a few actors on the TV Show *The Parkers* and that I should do extra work on there to earn my SAG card. Since most extra work was filmed during the day, this meant I had to drop out of school to free up my schedule. Doing extra work on *The Parkers* was a great experience. I met several people on set and struck up some lasting friendships like my boy, Jackie Long, who ended up making it on the big screen. I was excited for myself and the work I was putting in. I only made $100 before taxes an episode, but I was paying my dues like everyone else, so I didn't mind.

LaVassa had recommended that I lose weight because I was too thick for the camera. I was 215lbs and she felt that if I wanted to maximize all my options in the industry, I should get myself down to at least 180lbs. I trusted her opinion, so I joined

L.A. Boxing Club downtown.

I heard that getting a boxing trainer would cost a lot of money, but you could try your luck and tell a trainer you wanted to fight, and they would train you contingent of you turning pro for them, so that's what I decided to do.

One late afternoon in the gym I was doing my usual, heavy bag work, hoping to spark the interest of one of the old trainers. They usually sat together in one section as spectators, in hopes of finding a young new prospect.

This particular day, as I was unwrapping my hands, one of the old trainers with a no-nonsense face and a firm tone, walked up to me and said, "How you doing young man? My name is Coach Vernon."

I extended my hand and introduced myself. "Hi, my name is Sonny Weathers."

"I've been observing your routine the last couple of days, and I can tell that you have some athleticism, kid, and you're in decent shape," he continued. "You ever thought about boxing?"

I told him about my athletic background, and to my surprise, he asked if I was looking for a trainer and if I would be interested in training for the 2004 Olympics.

"From the looks of things, you got what it takes. What do you have to lose? I can make you into a world champion.

If you can dedicate your time and efforts, I'll commit mine to you. How's that sound?"

"Sounds good to me! Let's do it!" I exclaimed.

I didn't take him seriously, and I didn't have any intentions of fighting professionally, let alone training for something as major as the Olympics. But, he was adamant. I just wanted to get into shape and lose weight, but I figured I would see how far I could actually go with a real trainer.

After my first month of training consistently in the gym, I started to like it. Fighting was in my blood, so I never minded, but I had a new career in acting that I still had my eyes on. I stayed busy February and March, running 5 miles a morning, on set two days a week, and training in the gym three days a week, sometimes 3 to 4 hours a day. Working out and training hard was second nature to me, and Vernon appreciated my commitment to getting into boxing shape.

A month into my training Vernon put me in the ring with a pro who had been fighting for many years. I wasn't at all scared. When the bell rang, I jumped all over him like a hungry pit-bull who had been locked in a cage for months. I whooped him so bad he dropped to the floor a couple times. Both trainers had jumped in the ring to pull me off him.

"Vernon, you look like you got you a fighter. He can punch too," said one of the outside trainers while the others nodded in approval.

From that moment on, all the trainers called me "Champ" when I walked in the gym.

One Saturday in March, I went to visit my oldest sister LaVassa, who had made breakfast for me. This was actually the first time in a long while that we just sat and talked. We talked about my acting career and the goals she had for us. She told me that she was proud of me for staying diligent and never giving up after all I'd been through growing up, but she also told me she wasn't happy about me having a child out of wedlock. Her concern for me was that I got on my feet. This was a day that I'll never forget the glow she had on her face. It was almost prophetic. I could tell that she'd found her peace on earth and with God. I was glad that we were establishing a relationship, and I wanted to do everything I could to make her and everyone else who believed in me proud. There was still a lot of work to get done – first, get things right with my daughter's mom.

* * *

It wasn't at all a typical Monday. My mood was odd. I guess it was all the built-up frustration from everything going on in my life. I wasn't where I wanted to be - 25 years old and literally fighting for my livelihood.

I was in the gym, shadowboxing in the ring, and tears began pouring down my face. I guess you say I was having a mental meltdown. Vernon suggested that I take the rest of the day off to get myself together. So, I got dressed and left.

While driving to pick up my girlfriend from work, I got a call from my dad, which was weird. He called to tell me that LaVassa was on her way to the hospital because she was having difficulty breathing. I calmly said, "Okay."

I hung up the phone and began to cry again. I knew and remembered the tears I had cried before my brother died, and in that moment that same feeling took over my body. My girlfriend, who was now in the car with me, asked me why I was crying, and I told her, "I think LaVassa is about to die."

She yelled and asked, "Why would you say such a thing? I just think you need some counseling." She was trying to make light of the situation, but, she was probably right.

I couldn't explain it to her or anyone what I was feeling at the time because they would just think I was crazy. Deep down inside, I knew something wasn't right. I decided to go home, take a nap, and sleep it away.

Later that evening I woke up to my girlfriend's screams. When I came out of the room, she just stared at me with tears in her eyes and the phone in her hand.

I calmly asked, "Is it LaVassa?"

She nodded and kept crying. She said my dad was on the phone and that LaVassa had passed away. All the family was at Centinela Hospital - the same place where my brother had died.

I arrived at the hospital that evening with my entire family there trying my best to be strong for my mother and my sisters. Death is always sad, and the irony was that it was the only time our family got together.

It was odd for me because I had not spoken to my mom or the rest of my family until then, and I had to wear the face of strength when I needed it myself. I don't remember how I made it through that night. I was sick and felt like I was about to lose my mind. I was just existing and had to suppress all the pain I had in my life to maintain some level of normalcy. I have no doubt that God was with me during this time. Looking back there was no other way I could have survived the feelings of hurt and pain that took over me. This was one of the biggest mountains to climb of my journey – loss.

Just the thought of my brother lying on that gurney plagued me for so many years. I promised I would never look upon a loved one's deceased body again. So, I chose not to view LaVassa's body. I wanted to remember her just the way I knew her - her radiance, her sense of purpose and passion, her love, her smile. I wanted to remember when she told me she was proud of me. I wanted to remember when she told me she believed in me. I wanted to remember the last day I was with her and she told me she loved me.

The next day, I got up at 5:50A.M. and got dressed in my sweat pants, running shoes, hoodie sweater, beanie and Walkman. I ran and ran and ran, and it was as if I was the only person on the street. I was completely zoned out. I lived on 180th and Crenshaw at the time, and that morning I ran all the way to Pico and Fairfax nonstop with tears streaming down my face all the way to my grandma's house. All I remember was that I had made it to her front door and passed out from the heat and dehydration. I had run over 25 miles. I had never run that far in my life. I felt like I had an out of body experience. The Lord came to me and told me to be strong and that He was with me. He was the comfort I needed at that moment.

After LaVassa's funeral that Saturday, I never went back to *The Parkers* or acting. Instead I chose to take my frustration out in the boxing ring. I moved back to my grandma's. I didn't talk much the next few months, but I did wake up every morning and run. I found peace in running, and I needed all the peace I could get.

I ran 5 miles a day and finally got down to 185lbs. I kept working in the group home, and working there was like my therapy. I found strength in what some of the kids there were dealing with. Other than work and training, I kept to myself. It was what I needed to get my life back in order.

I also did tons of reading. I read everything from autobiographies and poems to self-help books. My peers and family always commended me for being mentally strong, but at this point in my life, the fight was completely out of me. My ambition and drive to live had been daunted by all that happened in my life. I knew better than to sit and sulk about my problems. I needed time, nevertheless, to relearn who I was inside, and reading helped me to rediscover that.

I had to remember that I was a child of God who's not defined by my faults and failures, and as long as I had air to breathe, I had the opportunity to change my life. But like all things, change was a challenge. I questioned where I was in my life and what I wanted to do with my life. I was working in a place making $8 an hour and training at a boxing gym with no real desire to have a boxing a career.

Working in the group home was rewarding, but I didn't see myself there forever. Boxing was cool too, but I realized being 25 and trying to turn pro was far-fetched. Going back to school was still an option, but starting over from junior college was another journey altogether. It was going to take me three years to get my bachelor's degree, and I felt time was not on my side now that I had a mouth to feed.

The kind of money I needed to get things right in my life was possible in boxing. My trainer continued to prepare me to try out for the 2004 Olympics as an amateur. I was going along with the plan, but the hard thing would be to convince my family to support this idea. I was living with my grandma at the time, but my life there was very unstable. If she needed to use my room for a client, I was back in the streets. I had to keep a positive attitude about trying out for the Olympics because I really didn't have too many other things going on at the time.

For the next few months boxing was my life. But, in the back of my mind, I knew I would have jumped ship if another opportunity came my way. Vernon had the plan, and

I had the time and not much else. In 2001, we began the journey to make the

2004 Olympic boxing team. It was great that he believed in my talents. I felt I owed him, and the least I could do was show up to gym every day. Besides, I had my brother and sister looking down on me from heaven and my daughter here who needed me.

Part of being a man means making decisions that weigh the balance of tomorrow today.

Chapter 11

9/11

September 11, 2001 was the spark I needed to motivate me in the ring. I was not only fighting for me, but for all the Americans who lost loved ones in the tragedy. I felt that my life represented a degree of will and strength that was necessary to stand on that Olympic podium and receive a gold medal.

Vernon and I decided to move to another gym location he thought would suit me best and provide the sparring I needed to reach our goals. We moved to Broadway Gym in Watts, CA, owned by Bill Slayton, a popular boxing trainer. Broadway Gym was full of young talent and old timers still competing. I was in the heart of my city and around all the hungry fighters in L.A. Whenever you fight as an amateur you are part of a team, and mine was Team Broadway.

My family had taken notice of my new-found passion and thought this could actually be the thing for me. Yes, I was older for a career in boxing, but I was still in great shape and willing. The more I competed, the more passion I developed for the sport. I often reflected on the time my father bought my first pair of red boxing gloves, but little did I know I would actually step into a real ring with a real opponent.

Everyone was excited for my first fight and I was in need of my family's support, so I invited everyone to come see me. I was so excited just to see everyone together for an occasion other than a funeral.

I didn't even have proper boxing gear when I fought that day. I wore some basketball shorts, Nike Air Max, and a Broadway Boxing Team shirt I owned with pride. My mom, dad, sisters, aunts and friends cheered me on as I walked into the ring. I wasn't nervous at all. I could have fought anyone that day.

Having my family there made me feel invincible. That was until my opponent walked into the ring, and I could hear all the cheers for me begin to go silent. My opponent was bigger and much more muscular than I was. I had weighed in at 179lbs and he was 200lbs and around 6'1. I took the fight against Vernon's will because I had my family showing up and I didn't want to let them down by not fighting. My original opponent saw me at the weigh in and backed out, and since the guy I fought didn't have an opponent to fight, I told Vernon to let me fight him. Of course, Vernon put up a protest that he was much bigger, but I didn't care. I trained hard and was ready.

After the introduction, I could see all the worried faces of my family and friends, I nodded with confidence that I had this. Besides I had fought bigger dudes in the streets and competed against bigger guys in football.

The first round started with me firing my jab and hitting him at will. I was doing a lot of moving. I guess one would say it was nervous energy but I hit him with everything - right hands, left hooks - but he kept coming. The round ended with a straight right hand that had his legs buckling and the crowd on their feet. I went back to the corner gasping for air. I was surprised he didn't go down because I had thrown punches darn near the entire round. I felt like I had given him everything I had.

In the second round, he came out roaring with me moving around the ring just to try and regain my breath from the previous round. He never really landed anything heavy that entire round, but I did connect big a few times, hurting him in the exchanges. However, I couldn't wait until the second round ended because I was already out of gas. Everyone had noticed I had punched myself out, and I was in survival mode. Thank goodness, I made it to the bell.

I was so tired Vernon wanted to stop the fight, but I demanded him not to. I could hear my Grandma CJ screaming the loudest for me to quit because I had been breathing so hard. But I came out the third round with my best boxing moves. I knew what I wanted to do, but my legs weren't responding. Finally, he caught up with me and ended up backing me into a corner and began wailing away. None of the punches landed, but his elbow ended up breaking my nose. The ref stopped the fight as soon as he saw the blood gushing out.

I lost the fight on a technical stoppage, yet I knew deep down inside he didn't beat me. But his hand was raised and that was that.

You can only imagine the looks on my family's faces. Everyone, including my dad, felt that boxing wasn't for me and that I should have given up after that day. In my head, I knew he didn't beat me. I ended up beating myself due to all the wasted punches and moving around. I just had to get back in the ring and keep at it.

The next time I fought that year was in the Golden Gloves tournament as a novice. This time I wasn't going to be fighting anyone out of my weight class, which would be easier for me to handle. In amateur shows, you can fight at whatever weight you or your coach think is comfortable, but during tournaments, you have to fight at your own weight class. I didn't invite my family to come as they had written off my boxing career.

I had three fights that tournament. I won my first two fights by decisions and made it to the finals, which I won by a second-round KO.

I stayed active the next couple of years. I fought in the Regional Pal Open Championships with only 8 fights and made it to the finals, but I lost to a fighter, by decision, who had over 100 amateur fights. I fought in the Blue and Gold Games and again lost in the finals by decision.

I also made it to the Regional Final in the Golden Gloves in 2003 and lost to the same fighter I fought in the Blue and Gold Games. Our final fight was a good one, however. He beat me in a close fight 4 points to 3, and if it were a pro fight, I would have won, because I dropped him in the first round. That fight gave me the momentum and confidence I needed in my next tournament.

The summer of 2003 I won my first minor title at, The "Boxers for Christ" Championships. The "Boxers for Christ" Championship was significant because my grandmother had just sold her apartment and moved to Las Vegas that week. It was a challenge trying to focus on training and wondering where I'd be living the next couple of weeks. I had to make my move in the amateurs that year, or else I would not qualify for a seat in the Olympic trials. If I qualified I would have been able to get a room and board stipend from the Amateur Boxing Association, which was what I needed so that I could focus on my training. I figured it was the only chance I had towards some type of financial liberation and notoriety in the sport.

It just so happened that Richard Steele, a famous boxing referee, was in attendance and was so impressed by my performances - 3 KO's in 3 fights, the last of which was a first round KO 15 seconds into the match - that he gave me his card and invited me to come to Vegas where he trained. This was pretty ironic considering that my grandma CJ had moved to Vegas. It now looked like I was going to do the same.

Even though I had won my first title, that didn't mean sponsorships were coming. Because my only support moved, I had to move with her if I was going to have the stability I needed to box.

When I moved to Vegas, I began my training at Richard Steele's Boxing Gym right away. The only good thing about moving to Vegas was getting a chance to meet so many fighters and people in the boxing world.

Vegas is the boxing mecca of the world, and the people of Vegas support their fighters, especially their amateurs. Moving there was like a breath of fresh air. I was able to eat and sleep boxing. My only setback was I didn't have Vernon with me who my grandmother had agreed could stay in the home she bought to finish our training together. He couldn't move because of his responsibilities in L.A., and he was upset with me for leaving. He didn't understand that I had to move or else I would have been in L.A. homeless.

I was training for the most part by myself until I decided to move to a gym my uncle recommended called Golden Gloves. Golden Gloves was run by world renowned trainer, Doc Broadus, who was known for taking George Foreman to the Olympics. At least there I was able to get sparring every day and have someone who worked with me. Doc was in his 80's and was too old to really train someone, but the old man did what he could and got me ready for State Police Athletic League. I won the state title in Nevada as a light heavyweight and went to Nationals where I lost in the second round by a close decision to the guy who made it to the finals.

It would have been nice to have won the tournament, but my chances of making it to the Olympics were fading quickly because I had not won a national title yet. I still had hopes of being invited to the Olympic trials, since I was one of the top amateur light heavyweights in the Nevada region. I had gained some experience in major tournaments on what to expect, so I was looking forward to the regionals in January 2004.

My hopes came to an end when I found out I wasn't allowed to represent Nevada for the Nationals because I was registered in L.A., which was against the rules. There went my hopes for the Olympics. On top of that, my girlfriend back home was pregnant and was getting ready to have my son. He was born on July 15, 2003 and I was home the next week. I moved in with my son's mom, and we got married a few months later.

I got a job, went back to school, and started training again with Vernon in early 2004. I fought amateurs for the last time by winning California State Police Athletic League Championships as a heavyweight before turning pro.

With hope still in sight of making it big in the pro ranks, there was no time for error, especially at the age of 28 with two kids and a wife. My wife was holding the bulk of the financial burden, and we weren't off to a good start. I promised her that if I lost a fight, I would give it up because it was taxing our home life and relationship.

I won my first pro fight by KO; however, it was hard trying to get fights, and the little money I made working part-time wasn't enough to support my family. Most of the fights that Vernon and I scheduled pulled out last minute, which again, was costing us money.

My marriage was starting to fail. She had supported me as best she could, and we tried to make us work as best as we knew how. I ended up quitting boxing in 2005 and went away to South Dakota in 2006 to play football in the National Indoor Football League (NIFL) thinking that some time apart and an extra $900 a week would help. I could make money playing football and working a full-time job on the side to help out my family. After a few months, I returned home with my wife and son. We thought that having another child would help fix us.

When my second daughter was born January 26, 2007, I was working in a group home making $9 an hour and going to school full-time. Everything that I had dreamt was over and had come to end. I was desperately trying to find it in my home life, but I just wasn't happy. By this time, I was at an all-time low. Everything in my life had failed. I lost my brother. I was put out of my house at 16. I had a broken leg, which meant no more baseball. Football didn't work. My sister died. Olympic hopes - fail. Pro boxing - time wasn't on my side. I could barely support my kids, and my marriage was headed to divorce court. I was at an all-time low. That was all my professional experience and education would allow me to do, and of course $9 an hour was not enough to support my family.

On my daughter's first birthday, out of desperation, I decided to join the military. I learned that part of being a man meant making decisions that weigh the balance of tomorrow today. I felt like I had exhausted all other possibilities, and I had to do something. The decision didn't happen overnight, but it was one of the best decisions I could have made in my life.

More than 2,300 military deaths took place during Operation Enduring Freedom.

Chapter 12

Salute

My National Guard recruiter was one of the most humble and honest men I had met. If it were not for him, I probably would not have joined the military. He was also raised in L.A. and had endured many trials and tribulations, so he could relate to the despair I was feeling at that time. He became my mentor and brother, and I trusted his guidance.

During this time, I was lost and lacked a real plan for my future. And once again, I was homeless and had no idea what I would do next or how I would support myself, let alone three children. But I did my best to remain positive through it all. Against my family and friends' wishes, I joined the National Guard in February 2007 and never looked back.

To civilians the military is an unknown world. One that we are aware exists somewhere out there, but no true understanding of what it's really like. Before most people step foot on a site, I can attest to the fact that many who enlist dread the monstrosity of basic training camp [and the military].

In my experience and probably like so many others, the horror stories began when I went to get my physical done at the Military Entrance Processing Station (MEPS), which is where everyone who wants to enter any branch of the military has to get their paperwork and physical completed. You meet people from all walks of life - some who have prior military service and are trying to re-enlist, others who have been there all day only to find out they will not be able to join, and then people like me, not really sure how they ended up in here in the first place. But somehow, we all managed to convince ourselves that this was the best decision.

Then the sense of doubt and fear looms because of the many uncertainties in the military world. My dad was a Vietnam vet, so I already lived through the ramifications of war. I knew that being in the military was not how Hollywood films portrayed it by any means. Though the war scenes in films minutely capture the disaster and death that occur during war, more than often these films fail to capture what happens after the war. The emotions, the pain endured for a lifetime when soldiers, families, and countries are left to find normalcy and peace again. Sometimes, normalcy and peace are never found. But, waiting around in the MEPS station made me think about my father more than I ever did before.

I wondered how trapped and hopeless he must have felt as he sat at the MEPS station getting ready to go off to war. Unlike myself, he was not given a choice to join the military. He was drafted. Though he was much younger than me when he got drafted, he was far more stable in life. I thought about how different he might have been had he not gone to Vietnam. As I sat there waiting for my name to be called, I remember feeling sympathetic towards my father's life-long addiction to drugs and alcohol for the first time in my life. I could not even imagine the horrific things he might have witnessed during his service in the military and all of life's heartbreaks that kept him frozen. It was not until that day, as a 32-year-old-man, that I was able to view my father through a different lens, one without anger nor judgment.

It's interesting how joining the military and sitting in MEPS caused me to reflect on the smallest details in my life. I suppose it was because my life and future was uncertain. After all, I made the choice that once I completed basic training, I would volunteer to do a tour in Iraq. My long-term goal was to eventually join a combative unit and impart my boxing skills to teach soldiers to defend themselves in pugilism. Though there was a strong possibility of death or becoming injured during the war in Iraq, I honestly didn't fear it. Growing up in L.A. during the 90's as a black man, I had to live day by day anyways.

The uncertainty of living to see another day - sadly to say - was something I'd become numb to. However, this time it didn't seem so destitute. I suppose I felt like I had some control over my destiny. For once, I actually saw a way to merge all my athletic and fighting experience with something that would allow me to become stable in more ways than one. I was excited about the possibilities and where and what I could do in the military.

After about four hours, I was told to sit in a section to get sworn in, and moments later I found myself standing in a room with about 20 other men and women with my right hand over my heart and my left hand raised. I was ready to embrace the unknown world of the military.

My departure to the airport for basic training was a lonely one because only my recruiter was there to see me off. I knew that this time around I had to take this journey alone. I was certain of that fact. My wife filed for divorce a month prior so I knew that part of my world was over. I had not been in contact with my parents or siblings for months. I felt so isolated from everyone I knew and loved and it was as if I were in a world all alone. I was drained emotionally and physically from all the fighting, struggling and disappointments in life, and I was relieved to be leaving L.A. I literally fell asleep before takeoff and did not wake until the plane landed in Oklahoma.

As instructed to do by my recruiter before I left, I walked outside and headed towards a white school bus. From a distance, I could see two individuals walking back and forth wearing military uniforms standing in front of a group of men. As I got closer, one of the men in uniforms was screaming, but I couldn't tell if it was directed to me or if he was screaming at the people in front of him. Then I realized that both men were drill sergeants and that he was in fact screaming, "Are you Weathers?"

I said, "Yes, sir," as I ran within a few steps of the group.

142

He went up another octave, "Sir? Who you calling sir, boy?" And he was literally standing directly in my face as to where I felt his spit hit my nose.

For a split second, my instinct was to ask him who he was calling boy; but then I remembered my recruiter told me everything and every moment in basic training was a test, so I just stayed quiet.

He yelled, "My name is Drill Sergeant Mosby." As he took a few steps back and addressed the entire group of men, he continued, "And my sole purpose for the next 12 weeks is to make this experience a nightmare for you fools. Some of you idiots won't even make it past 2 weeks, so find comfort in the fact that the person to your left and right won't be there."

After a few more minutes of loud and emasculating threats, we were instructed to "hurry up and load our luggage onto the white chariot." As we sat on the bus, the entire ride was practically silent. I suppose everyone wanted to avoid screams from Drill Sergeant Mosby or his battle buddy, Drill Sergeant Cross.

I did not care what any drill sergeant could have said to me because I doubted anything or anyone there would be as close to the madness I grew up with. I knew I was mentally strong and could endure anything I put my mind to, and I was devoted to getting through this test. I was just happy we had air on the bus and we were not standing out in the summer heat.

143

On the drive to the base, all I could think about was how badly I missed my children and being with them every day. I knew that I would not see them for a very long time, so I quickly changed thoughts because I could feel myself getting into my emotions. I knew I had no time for anything that could deter me from completing basic training successfully. I was on my way to uncover a world I knew very little about, and much like everyone else I felt anxious, excited and nervous at the same time. I had to save what little energy I had left. I was fighting for my life and a chance to become the man I wanted to be.

After arriving on post, we joined what seemed to be an assembly line to acquire all our military issued gear. The day was followed with much more screaming and rushing for us only to get back to a group of guys all standing around waiting to be told their next move. From the looks of things, I was one of the oldest in my company. Drill Sergeant Mosby even joked that, "I had him by a few years."

As we headed back to the barracks with our newly issued military gear, we all toed one of the two lines that started from the first bunk and ended at the last bunk. After everyone's names were called out, Drill Sergeant Mosby instructed us to stare the man standing directly in front of us in the eye because he would be our battle buddies for the duration of our stay. I've always heard in sports that a team is only as strong as their weakest link.

Somehow, I ended up being battle buddy with a young 19-year-old kid who had already managed to stand out from everyone else, but for all the wrong reasons. Instead of calling him our company's weakest link, let's just say that private Nicks would be the reason I had to do so many extra pushups and so much running. He would also turn out to be one of the most intelligent persons I'd ever met.

Nicks was short, 5'4", uncoordinated and overweight for his height. He was a Caucasian kid from Griswold, Iowa, and it was clear that he'd never been in any competitive sports. I often wondered how he even passed the basic requirements to get into the military. Though he didn't have one drop of human or military bearings, he did have heart.

I learned so much during the next 12 weeks of basic training. I learned a lot about people and how we have more things in common than perception would lead you to believe. I rediscovered many of my strengths and weaknesses. Once I learned to avoid having to be told anything twice and to keep a low profile, it was pretty much smooth-sailing. I had already been in shape, so the physical aspect of it was not my hardest challenge. The most challenging part was being in charge of a bay of 50 men and getting everyone on the same page - mostly my battle buddy. After many nights of breaking up fights between the guys in the barracks and giving advice after 'lights out,' I learned that the best thing I could do for the guys was to be myself and lead by example. A part of that was to share my experiences as a man, which for the first time I was able to share freely.

Though my battle buddy had scored a perfect score on the ASVAB exam to get into the military, he sucked at the physical aspect of training. But I managed to help him get to standard all the way around. He was what people in the military called "ate up." He was always the last one to complete anything, and to make it worse, he had a know-it-all attitude that always landed the both of us in trouble with our drill sergeant.

I ended up graduating and receiving Soldier of the Cycle Award, and my battle buddy received the Most Improved Soldier Award. I was prouder for him than I was for myself, seeing all the hard work he'd put in. Graduation was an auspicious moment because for the first time I felt like I had completed something all on my own. Everyone had their families there but me. If it wasn't for my battle buddy Nick introducing me to his family as his mentor and big brother, I would have been all alone. I spent my graduation day with them. They treated me to dinner and made me feel like part of the family.

I hadn't spoken to any of my family members the entire time there. Nonetheless, I was happy in that moment and excited again about my future.

Looking back, basic training was what I needed to get myself together. After three months and as planned, I volunteered to go to Iraq. I was excited to leave that fall, and being straight out of basic had me prepared and ready. I reported to Fort Dix, New Jersey, a mobbing site for National Guard and Reserve component soldiers. I put my name on a volunteer list, and I was chosen by a Special Forces Unit because of my high marks from Basic Training. There I met up with my unit I was to deploy with, but first, I had to go through two weeks of Desert Training to get trained up on mission protocol. Everything was going according to plan.

Life has a way of issuing its own cards for you. I didn't make it to my final destination in Iraq because I got injured preparing in a convoy exercise preparing for a mission. I was sent to Ft. Lewis, Washington for a week to have my injury evaluated by the medical department of the Army. When I returned to Ft. Dix, I was reassigned to WTU, a unit for injured soldiers. After being in WTU for a few months, I went back to Ft. Lewis again to determine if I would remain in the military.

I was medically discharged from the Army in August the following year, around the same time my grandmother had passed. I didn't get a chance to make it to her funeral, and I guess it was best that I didn't. I really didn't have it in me to grieve, but I knew she was in a better place, and since we were so close, me not being there during her last days only gave me the feeling that she was still there.

Families that pray together stay together.

Chapter 13

The Mark of a Soldier

My whole reason for wanting to go overseas was to meet up with a unit with whom I could share active duty. My ambitions of joining an Army combative team and train fighters in pugilism were halted. Nothing worked out according to my plan, and I was about to return home injured and probably viewed as a failure to my family once again. But, everything happens for a reason.

While on my way home from Fort Dix, I got an email from my battle buddy's mom letting me know that Nicks was killed in an IED bombing in Fallujah, Iraq.

He didn't get to see 20 years old, but he knew his purpose and pursued it. All he wanted to be was a soldier like his father and both grandfathers, and that he was. He always tried to improve himself as a man and as a soldier, which is all we can expect - just work to be better.

I admired the close bond he had with his family. They were a small family - mother, father, four uncles and two aunts, and grandparents on both sides. He would talk about how they used to argue and fight amongst themselves, and being the only grandchild, he had to be the peacemaker.

During the holidays, he would be responsible for bringing the families together and making it through the holiday with no drama. One thing about his family, being that they were from a small town, a population of only 1,000, they had grown up together as kids and had formed an unbreakable closeness.

They were really known as the fighters of the town, and if an "outsider" messed with one of them, they would have hell to pay because his mom, dad, four uncles, two aunts and sometimes the grandparents would take care of business. They could have just been in a family bustle between themselves, but those family squabbles didn't change the love and loyalty they had for each other. I could feel it when I met them. Sitting at the dinner table going back and forth with laughter then arguments, arguments then laughter. But, when they bowed their heads in prayer, everybody was on one accord - for that moment anyway.

Just thinking about my grandma, CJ, Nicks and his family made me want to bring my family closer. Life is short and can be taken from us at any moment. There's no need to be holding grudges because it's not healthy. I decided on my return home to get the family together for Christmas dinner at my Aunt Boosie's house...my treat. She was the cook in the family, and everybody loved Auntie Boosie.

I invited everybody to come down. One thing black folks don't do is turn down food, so you know everyone showed up!

My mom, dad (who I hadn't seen in years), my sisters, aunts, uncles, and my children were all there. Under one roof. Like the Christmas dinners we had when I was a kid. When we spent hours listening to the elders tell stories.

When kids could barely control themselves of the excitement of "Santa" coming. When all the kids sat at the small table while the adults sat at the "big" table. When we held hands while the men of the family prayed over the meal. Now it was my turn...

"...Let us pray. Lord, I thank you for this gathering on this auspicious occasion – the coming together of our family during the Christmas season. We thank you for the food we're about to receive and for those who prepared it. And Lord, bless those who are less fortunate and have none to receive. We thank you for what you do in each of our lives. We thank you for all things. Amen," I prayed.

Holidays have a way of bringing about joy and togetherness. Everyone smiling. Everyone laughing. Everyone's belly full. At the end of the day, that's what it's all about. Family.

* * *

I recall feeling like a hamster on a wheel for so many years. With no end or resolution in sight. It was as if I was just existing and trying to survive, but never really living. Yet, a part of me knew that somehow everything I had done and experienced would have to be used to my advantage or someone else's one day. I have to admit that I had a lot of great moments throughout my life, but until recently, they were all overshadowed by the 21 years I had been struggling to find my way. When I left my mother's house at 16, I had no idea it would have taken so long to recapture my freedom, but I never stopped searching.

As long as we have breath in our bodies, we have a fighting chance towards life and to change. So, I can only be optimistic about what life has in store for me in the future. If we fail to renew the lens in which we view the world, we will only see failure and feel pain. Though this life may seem unfair and can appear to always hand us the short end of the stick, all we can really do is see things out to the end and learn to evaluate and appreciate the journey and moments in between.

The peace that I have today came as a result of me taking myself through this journey to uncover who I was and who I am. It was my willingness to trust God, my instincts, and the process. It came about not because I had many regrets I wanted to rewrite, but because I knew if I had changed one slight instance in my life, the me today may not have been possible. For that reason alone, I would do it all again. I believe we will receive our greatest lessons, develop the strength and character needed to take us through the next phase of our lives if we remain open for change throughout life's journeys. Ultimately, we are required to forgive and become grateful for it all - as this is the never-ending journey to wellness – peregrination.

Epilogue

Oh, I almost forgot. My older cousin Michael, who was like a big brother to me as a child, well, he was at the Christmas dinner too. We spent the entire night reminiscing on the old days and catching up as if we had never been apart.

Michael was a successful businessman who ran a nutraceutical company, among other business ventures. He mentioned that he had heard about all of my accomplishments from other family members, but he could never get in contact with me directly. He told me he was proud of me for all I had done and for never quitting on my dreams.

For many years, my grandmother CJ was the only person in my life who always encouraged me to aspire to do something great; it felt good to hear another family member acknowledge my efforts now that she had passed.

I told him that I was thinking about going back to school to finish the few classes I needed to get my bachelor's degree and to grad school after that. In the midst of me talking about school, he told me that my life and experiences would make me a perfect fit for his company. He then asked if I would be interested in a position after I graduated. I told him I would take him up on that opportunity and that I would call him as soon as I finished. We exchanged numbers and from that day, we stayed in touch.

Needless to say, my cousin delivered on his promise and a month after graduating with my master's, his company paid for me to relocate to their office in Atlanta. I was given a company car and signed a two-year lease on a condo. Just like that, I was on a path of stability for once in my life. This time I was armored with confidence and a compelling drive to be a man my children, family, and loved ones could look up to – the man I've been on this journey to become.

* * *

My ability to level up through my many transitions was not subsequent or by chance. I consistently read and elevated my mind through self-help and motivational books. As Louis Pasteur once said, "Chance favors only the prepared mind." I committed to healthy eating and keeping my body intact. And most importantly, I stayed in meditation and constant prayer with the Creator. No matter the situation, I kept my mind, body, and spirit in sync…SUCCESS.

About the Author

Sonny Weathersby AKA "Coach Sonny" is a California- native, born and raised in the inner cities of Los Angeles. He received his Master's Degree in Public Administration and is currently working on his Doctoral Degree in Psychology - Health Psychology. He presently serves as the CEO of Big League Publishing and Coach Sonny LLC, a motivational speaker, and a certified life coach. He also has a nonprofit organization, What It Takes, that focuses on preparing at-risk youth for college and beyond.

Visit **www.SonnyWeathersby.com** for more information about *Peregrination: The Journey to Wellness.*